Sammy in France

Single Wide Female Travels
Book 1

By

Lillianna Blake

DEDICATION

To all women out there dreaming of travel.
If it's something you want, go for it! ☺

TABLE OF CONTENTS

CHAPTER 1

I shifted the strap of my bag on my shoulder. It was biting into the soft skin underneath the sleeve of my shirt. The line moved forward inch by inch.

"Max, are you sure that there's nothing wrong?" I tried to see past the crowd of people to the gate of the plane.

"It's fine, just too many people to get on at one time." Max slid his hand into mine. He squeezed it gently.

Sometimes I thought Max had magical powers in his hands. Every time he touched me or held my hand, everything that once bothered me disappeared. As if to prove my theory right, the line moved forward. I tried to focus on the next leg of the trip. I wasn't afraid of planes, but I didn't relish the idea of the take-off.

"This is the first time I'm flying out of the country."

"Me too." Max ruffled his hair. "It's exciting and a little intimidating."

"I just wish we could get on there and get settled." I

yawned. "I could use a little nap."

As the crowd filed onto the plane, I could hear bits and pieces of the conversations around me. They were mostly in French. Max and I had both taken French in college, but he seemed to have a better memory for it than I did after so many years. I could pick up words here and there, but I was hoping to be able to hold a conversation by the time we'd spent a few weeks in France. The thought was pushed from my mind as I took my first step onto the plane. I smile at the flight attendant who greeted me. I was moments away from relaxation.

When I turned the corner, I found a congested aisle and had to take a deep breath to calm my nerves. Everyone seemed to be cramming their bags wherever they could find a space.

"Excuse me, excuse me, I'm so sorry." I tried to wedge my way down the aisle with the two carry-on bags I had strapped over my shoulder. It wasn't as if I could pack lightly. I wasn't just going across the country—I was going across the world.

"Here, let me take that." Max reached back to take one of the bags from me, then he hoisted it above his head and slid it into the compartment over the seats. "And the other." He held out his hand for it.

I tried to swing it into his grasp, but as I did, it grazed the shoulder of a woman who was already seated.

"Oh! Watch it! This outfit cost me well over one thousand dollars!"

"I'm sorry, it was an accident. I don't think it hurt your blouse."

"You don't think so? But you don't know, do you? In fact, you don't know anything at all about the exquisite material that went into creating this garment. So maybe you could be more careful where you swing your bag."

I took a slow breath and did my best to remain polite. "I'm sorry, the aisles are narrow."

"Not for me—maybe for someone like you." She lifted her chin and narrowed her eyes. "Maybe you should have gotten on a jumbo jet."

I stared at her. Had I really heard what I just heard? Could a grown woman truly be that cruel?

"There's no need for that." Max turned to face the woman. "Do I need to get a flight attendant over here?"

"Max, stop." I met his eyes. "I can handle this." I cleared my throat and looked straight into the woman's eyes.

"I'm sorry that you feel so insecure about your body that you feel the need to cover it in *garments* that cost enough money to feed several poor children. I hope that one day you'll realize your own beauty—from the inside out. Then you may find some peace in the world around you and tolerance for those of us that may struggle with the ability to be perfect. Now I'm going to find my seat, and I hope that you will respect our fellow passengers enough to let this minor incident go."

The woman stared up at me with wide eyes and

tightened lips. From the way her hands curled into fists I thought she might punch me. Instead, she turned her head toward the window and ignored me.

Max smiled at me as he guided me to our seats.

"I'm proud of you. You handled that woman better than I ever could."

"I hope I wasn't too rude." I sighed as I sat down in the aisle seat.

"You should have been rude. That woman needs to learn how to be a decent human being."

"Am I showing her that by biting back, though? The remark about her clothes was rather cruel."

"It's rather true. I'm sure that there are women that wear expensive clothing because they love it, but I'm betting that woman wears it because it makes her feel better than other people."

"Maybe." I shifted in my seat. Every time I moved, my body felt more out of place. The seat was roomy and cushioned, but my body did not cooperate.

"Comfortable?" Max looked over at me.

"Yes." I smiled.

The truth was, my bottom was already numb.

CHAPTER 2

I stared hard at the seat in front of me and tried not to think about how high in the air we would be in the next few minutes.

"Are you nervous?" Max smiled.

"Oh no, not at all. Flying is one of the safest ways to travel—far safer than driving in a car or even taking a train. I'm sure we'll be just fine."

"I am too, but that's not what I meant. I meant are you nervous about starting the book tour?"

I rested my head back against the seat and closed my eyes. "Things have been so crazy I haven't really had time to get nervous."

"I know. That going-away party was wild, wasn't it?"

"Wild isn't exactly how I'd describe it. I just want to know what made Stephanie think that a stripper was appropriate for a going-away party." I laughed and then covered my mouth quickly to muffle the sound.

"I'm pretty sure that stripper was more for her than it was for you. Still, it was quite entertaining when your mother offered up a few singles."

"Okay, I have to agree, that was very entertaining." I shook my head. "I never saw that one coming."

"I just can't believe we actually got it all done. There was so much to do. I really didn't think that we'd get through it all."

It was my turn to squeeze his hand as I met his eyes. "I never had any doubt. We make a great team, after all."

"That's for sure. But getting the house ready to rent out was a bit more than I thought we could handle."

"We did it. Now we're starting our year-long journey of exploring the world. What could be better than that?"

"A year to spend with you?" He smiled. "Nothing could be better than that."

I snuggled close to him and closed my eyes. "Let me know when it's time for take-off."

"Sammy." Max slid the window shade up.

I looked through the window at clear blue sky and puffy white clouds.

"Wow! We're already in the air?" I stared out with awe as the buildings below the plane grew smaller and smaller.

"It's going to be an amazing ride, Sammy. I have to say, I feel darn lucky to get to spend it with you."

"I can't wait to see the world with you. I'm going to take a million pictures!"

"I don't doubt that." Max laughed. "I just hope you remember to get some writing done in between."

"Oh, don't you worry, Max, I'm not going to forget about that at all. It's such an honor to be able to do this book tour. I just can't believe this is happening. It feels like I won the lottery or something."

"Why do you think that is?"

"I guess because I have everything I could ever want."

"No. I mean, why do you think things changed so much? It seems to me that the moment you started believing in yourself and following your passion, everything fell into place."

I cringed at his words. "Trust me, it wasn't that simple or easy. I've read so many books that promised if I just acted happy, I would be happy. But it took a lot more than that. I had to truly embrace myself—who I am—all of me, not just the fake-it-on-the-surface me." I wrapped my arm around his. "But it was well worth the work and the wait."

"I hope so." He kissed the tip of my nose. "It was a beautiful thing to witness your confidence grow. I've been waiting for it for years. To be honest with you, I think I could use a little of that journey myself. I'm hoping to be able to grow and expand a bit on our trip."

"Oh, that's wonderful." I stared at him for a long moment. I noticed that the corners of his mouth twitched. His eyes shimmered the way they did when something amused him. "You're talking about food, aren't you? You're talking about expanding your midsection."

"The other stuff too." He laughed. "There's so much delicious food to try! How could we not indulge a little?"

"Max, I'm going on this book tour to show that losing weight is possible when you heal your whole self. How will I be able to keep a straight face if I know I've just eaten a plate full of crepes?"

"You don't have to eat the whole plate, though. I mean, everything in moderation, right?"

I frowned. Everything in moderation had rarely worked for me. One bite was all it ever took to send me on a binge that I couldn't come back from. As a result, I'd learned to cut certain foods from my life pretty much completely.

"I don't know."

"Hey, I didn't mean to upset you."

"You can eat whatever you want."

"But that's not what I want—not just to eat anyway. I want to share the experience of the taste, the flavor, the texture of the food with you. I want to know what your opinion is on a dish that neither of us has ever eaten. Can't you fit it into your diet plan? I don't want to be anything but supportive, but this is an opportunity that most people only get once in a lifetime."

"You're right. I didn't really think about it like that. I'll do my best to keep an open mind about trying new things, no matter the calorie count. Alright?" I smiled at him.

"I'll believe it when I see it." He winked at me and then settled into his seat. "I'm going to get some rest. I'm sure I'll need it on this adventure."

As Max fell asleep I gazed past him out the window of the plane. The assortment of colors in the sky reminded me of a beautiful painting, even though the sensation of soaring so far above the ground also inspired tension in my jaw.

As I flew over parts of the world I'd never been to, I wondered if this would be a mistake.

Could Max and I really work together? Would it put too much strain on our marriage?

CHAPTER 3

I plugged my headphones into my phone and turned on the language program. I was immersed in the lovely lilt of the French language. I listened to the word spoken and then whispered it quietly. I didn't pay attention to the English translation, as I was only interested in calming my nerves. With every word I spoke, I took a deep breath. I imagined myself in a beautiful French cafe surrounded by conversations in French. As my mind drifted into a more peaceful state, I continued to repeat the words. I didn't pay attention to pronunciation, as it was more of a meditative exercise.

All of a sudden, out of nowhere, the soft surface of a pillow connected with my face. In my shock, I immediately felt that it was flung at me with the intention of inflicting pain. My eyes shot open. I pulled my headphones off and looked over at Max. At first I thought he must have been the one to throw the pillow, because who else would have the nerve? But Max was sound asleep.

I looked across the aisle. Many of the other

passengers were sleeping as well, but one had her arms crossed and a harsh glare fixed in my direction. I realized it was the same woman whose shoulder I'd brushed earlier with my bag. I was so stunned that I confronted her before I could make a better choice.

"Did you throw this pillow at me?"

"Yes, I did." She narrowed her eyes.

"That's pretty childish, don't you think?"

"Maybe. But so is repeating words in a language that you do not understand. I should not have to listen to such vulgar language. You weren't exactly quiet about it."

"Vulgar? It's a language program. It's so that I can communicate with people in France."

"If you try to talk to people like that in France, you'll be kicked right out. I can promise you that."

"What do you mean?"

"I don't know what kind of language program you're using, but the things that you were saying were nearly criminal and not appropriate in mixed company."

"That's nonsense." I frowned. "But for the sake of peace I will just listen to it."

"For the sake of your personal safety in the streets of France, you should check that program and make sure that it's not malfunctioning. Now, may I have my pillow?"

I stared at her hard for a moment, then I tucked the pillow under my head and closed my eyes.

I heard her call for a flight attendant to get her

another pillow and did my best not to smile.

After a few minutes, I looked at my phone. I had downloaded the program in a rush and hadn't really read the information about it. As I read it over, I was horrified to discover that I'd downloaded what I thought was one hundred French phrases, but it was actually one hundred sexy French phrases. As I read over some of the English translations of what I'd repeated—apparently louder than in the whisper I'd intended—I sank down in my seat.

I glanced over at an older man who sat an aisle up from me. He winked when he caught my eye. I lowered my eyes fast and tried not to think about what his opinion of me might be.

Yet again I doubted whether I'd made the right decision.

The subtle sound of Max's snore reminded me that I wasn't alone. But that didn't stop my mind from spinning. I closed my eyes to try to quiet it.

I took a deep breath and filled my belly with it. Then I held it for a few seconds before I released it. The release caused a sudden squeak to escape my throat. The woman in the aisle across from us looked over with a raised eyebrow. I smiled and placed my fingers against my lips as politely as I could.

It was easy to believe that the book tour would be a great idea, when it was just that—an idea. Now that it was about to become a reality—my new reality—I had to face the truth that I'd completely left my comfort zone behind.

In the past few months, I'd left my comfort zone behind about a lot of things. I was familiar with the fear and dread that welled within me. That didn't change the fact that it threatened to choke me as I tried to take another deep belly breath.

What was I thinking? How could I talk Max into renting out his home and joining me on tour? Now not only was my life, success, and future on the line, his was as well.

I looked over at him as he slumbered with such a calm expression on his face. He had no idea what was about to happen to him. I could only hope that I would be able to uphold my end of the deal and market the books well.

The B.I.G. *Girls Club* series had started out strong, but this was an entirely new market. I wondered for the millionth time who would buy my book in France. My impression of French women came from what I saw on the covers of fashion magazines. They were waif-like, without a flaw in sight. How would I fit in there with my thick frame? I'd reached a weight that I was comfortable with in time for the wedding, but it still fluctuated and there was nothing about me that was waif-like.

At some point I drifted off to sleep.

The next thing I experienced was the jolt of the landing gear as it struck the runway. I gasped and sat up.

Max took my hand and squeezed it. "It's alright.

We're here. I thought about waking you, but you looked so peaceful." He leaned over to give me a quick kiss on my nose.

"I was." I laughed. "Not so much any more."

"Sammy, we're here! We're in France!" Max smiled so wide that I had to smile back.

CHAPTER 4

Once we were free to file off of the plane, I waited until the woman in the expensive blouse was gone. Then Max grabbed our bags and began to head down the aisle. I noticed the older man that had winked at me still sat in his seat. I wondered if he might need help to get his bag, then I reminded myself that the flight attendants would help him if he needed it.

As I walked past him, he reached out and pinched the curve of my bottom. I yelped and jumped against Max's back. Max tumbled into an empty seat.

"Sammy!" He looked up at me. "What are you doing?"

"That man pinched my bottom!" My cheeks flared red. The man winked again and made a pinching movement with his fingers.

"Move out of the way, let me get to him!" Max stood up, ready to defend my honor.

I grimaced and put a hand on his chest. "It's okay, really. I might have propositioned him—by accident." I thought about the phrases I'd repeated.

"Huh?"

"It's a long story."

Max glared at the man for a moment and then nodded.

We continued down the aisle and made our way off the plane. Once we were by the gates, the next step was to find our baggage.

I held tight to Max's hand as we experienced the force of the crowd. It seemed that everywhere we tried to stop and figure out where to go next, we were in someone's way.

After being shuffled around the gate area for some time, Max and I finally made it to baggage claim. It was a bit like being in the middle of a rock concert, with people waving and pushing to get to the front. Once we had all of our bags Max tilted his head toward the front of the airport."

"Let's get out of this madhouse."

"Yes! The sooner the better!"

I kept an eye out for Grandpa Pinchy as we moved through the crowd and made it to the front of the airport.

"How many people do you think are here right now?" My eyes widened as I looked at the crowd piled at least three people deep at the doors of the airport. Some had just arrived, while most surged toward the curb outside of the airport.

"I can tell you that we're never going to get a taxi in this madness." Max frowned and tried to pull his phone out of his pocket. When he reached for it, one of the bags he'd slung over his shoulder slid free and landed hard on the floor.

I reached down to grab the bag, but as I reached for it, I didn't notice that the zipper was open a bit. When I yanked the bag up off the floor, the zipper opened the rest of the way. The contents of the bag spilled all over the floor. This wouldn't have been so bad, if this particular bag hadn't been the one that contained all of my toiletry items.

My deodorant skidded across the floor while my bag of razors scattered in all directions. Max and I chased down the items while at the same time we dodged the ever-present crowd of people.

Once we had everything back in the bag, Max met my eyes with a half smile. "So far so good, right?"

"I don't know." I shook my head. "It seems like everything is going wrong."

"Not true. The plane landed safely and we're together."

My mood lifted. Max always knew how to make me feel better.

As we walked out of the airport with our arms linked together, I forgot about the crowd and the angry woman on the plane. This was a fresh slate, an opportunity for me to experience a new country. I wanted to have the best attitude I could possibly have.

At just the moment we stepped onto the sidewalk, a

taxi pulled up and beeped its horn. The driver then parked and stepped out of the taxi.

"Welcome!" He smiled at both of us.

Max looked over at me with a raised eyebrow. "Well, that was unexpected."

The driver took a few of the bags from Max and carried them to the back of the taxi as he called over his shoulder, "Cateline sent me."

Max followed him with the rest of our luggage.

Once the bags were stowed, the driver opened the door for us. "Let's get you to your room so that you can both get some rest."

As I got into the car, I bit into my bottom lip. It was hard to believe that Cateline would go to such lengths for us. It was a gentle reassurance that this really was going to be an amazing tour.

Max slid into the car beside me and took my hand. He gave it a light squeeze and met my eyes. "Welcome to France, my love."

I almost answered him with one of the inappropriate French phrases I'd memorized but caught myself before I did. Instead, I rested my head on his shoulder and gazed out at the beautiful scenery that we passed.

Even though there were many things similar to the city I was accustomed to, there was so much that reminded me I was in France. The architecture was intricate and romantic. There were many restaurants and specialty shops—but the sidewalks were the same, filled with people headed to their destinations.

It was surreal to imagine that, not long ago, I'd walked down a similar sidewalk in a completely different country. Since I'd always focused on my day-to-day living, I'd never really thought about what people in other places were up to. It was fun to think that our lives might not be so different even though there were miles that separated us.

Maybe this was one of the reasons why many women here seemed to be identifying with my books. No matter what country we lived in, our lives were bound to be similar—filled with insecurities, hopes for something more, and strong desires to be loved by ourselves and others.

The thought of connecting with women around the world over these topics made me smile with the excitement of it all.

CHAPTER 5

The taxi dropped us off at the bed and breakfast. As the driver pulled away, I wondered if I should chase him down. One look at the place, and I wasn't so sure that it was the right for us. I'd stayed in a bed and breakfast before, so I knew not to expect a hotel, but this one looked more old than quaint, and more run-down than authentic.

"Are you sure this is the place?" I paused at the end of the sidewalk and stared up at the looming building. It was brick and three stories tall. The front of the building looked like it had had some weather damage or maybe something had actually struck it—some of the bricks were crumbling.

There wasn't much of a garden, but what was there was scraggly and brown, as if it hadn't been tended in some time. It gave the impression of an abandoned building rather than a bed and breakfast.

Max checked the sign and nodded. "This is it. Maybe it's nicer on the inside."

I could tell that his positive attitude was a little forced.

I nodded, picking up two of the bags.

When we reached the door, it swung open before either of us had a chance to knock.

"Hello! Hello!"

The cheerful tone of the woman's voice was enough to make my heart leap. Wild silver curls sprung from her head in all different directions. There was a tiny pink bow clipped to the curve of her bangs.

"Henry! Henry, they're here!"

I looked over at Max, whose smile faltered.

Behind the woman a tall thin man walked up to the door.

"How wonderful. Let me take those." He tried to take the bags from me.

"Oh no, it's fine. I can get them." To me he looked far too frail and thin to be able to carry my bags.

"Young lady, give me those bags this instant." Henry fixed me with a stare that reminded me of my fifth grade math teacher.

I gulped and handed over the bags. To my surprise, he handled them just fine.

The entrance of the bed and breakfast was narrow and oddly angled. It felt a bit like walking into a funhouse at a carnival. Then the hallway opened up to a wide circular room. On one side of the room there was an old piano along with an assortment of overstuffed furniture. On the other, there was a long bar covered with knickknacks. I assumed it was once used to serve drinks, but now there were so many little glass bears that there was no room to sit.

"Let's get you settled in, and then if you'd like, we have tea and biscuits for you. Your room is on the third floor—Oh, and I'm Poppy. My husband is Henry." She called over her shoulder.

"Nice to meet you. We're Samantha and Max." I looked over at Max, who was grinning at me. "Are there many other guests?"

I followed behind Poppy as she made her way up the stairs. She hung on to the railing so tightly that her knuckles turned white. I braced myself with each step I took in case I needed to catch her. Behind me, Max followed close, and behind him, Henry lumbered along with the bags.

"No other guests—just you two, so you'll get special attention!"

The landing for the second floor was filled with life-size dog statues. At first sight, I thought one was real. The dogs were all different kinds of breeds.

"Are you a collector?" I asked as we reached the third floor.

"Oh, those are to remember all of our pets." Poppy laughed.

That left me a little unsettled. "They're not the actual pets, are they?"

"Oh, heavens, no. They're just statues. It's nice to still feel like they are around."

The third floor had an old gold-colored carpet. There were four doors along the short hallway.

"Oh, Poppy, let them get into their room and get some rest. They don't want to hear about our beloved pets."

"Fine, fine. She asked!" Poppy swung the door open and stepped back from it. "There's extra bedding in the closet, soap in the bathroom, and some chocolates on your pillows."

"Don't eat the chocolates!"

"Oh, hush, Henry, they're fine!" Poppy pulled the door shut behind her as she argued with her husband.

I looked at Max with a lopsided smile.

Max shook his head. "They're a little strange, huh?" He peered at the chocolates on the pillows.

"Maybe. I think they're sweet. Do you think we'll be like that fifty years from now?"

"I hope not!" He laughed. Then he turned and swept his arm around my waist. "But I do know that we'll still be together. I'll still think that you're the most beautiful woman in the world. But, and I can't stress this enough, we will *not* have any dog statues."

"Maybe just one." I sat down on the end of the bed. The blanket was thick and the mattress was firm. I looked forward to a good night's sleep after the plane trip.

"I'm going to take a shower. Want to join me?" Max opened the bathroom door. Before I could answer he turned to look at me. "Maybe that's not such a good idea."

"Why?" I stood up and poked my head inside. The bathroom was large enough, aside from the shower stall, which looked just big enough for one average-sized person. "Oh yes, I don't think that would work." I laughed. "You go ahead. I'm going to get a few things unpacked."

As Max turned the shower on and tried to wedge himself inside, I turned back to our bags on the floor. After the incident at the airport I wanted to make sure that nothing was missing.

As I sorted through the items, I heard my phone ring. I heard it, but I didn't see it. With the bags spread around on the floor and piles of clothes here and there, it was hard to place where the ring was coming from.

I stood up to hear it better. When I did, I spotted the phone on the end of the bed. I lunged for it but one of the suitcases I'd moved was in my way. I caught my foot on the handle, spun in a complete circle, and landed on my back across the bed.

Out of breath, I grabbed for the phone. I meant only to see who it was but my finger slid across the screen as I picked it up.

CHAPTER 6

"Hello, Samantha?"

I recognized Cateline's voice right away. I didn't want the heavy breaths I was gulping down to give her the wrong impression.

"I'm here, I'm here. I'm so sorry. I was trying to get to the phone before it hung up, and I tripped over my suitcase." The truth popped out of me before I could think it through. It certainly didn't paint a very professional picture of me.

"Oh dear, are you okay?"

I bit into my bottom lip to keep myself from crying out as I rubbed at the curve of my big toe. "Yes, I'm fine."

"Was the car there to pick you up at the airport?"

"Yes, it was. Thank you so much for that."

"And is the bed and breakfast okay for you? A friend recommended it; I haven't been to it myself."

I swept my eyes over the small room, nodding my head. "Sure, it's great."

"Wonderful. I'd like to meet with you around nine in

the morning tomorrow, if that will work for you?"

"Absolutely I'll be there. I'm looking forward to meeting you."

"I'm looking forward to meeting you as well. I can't wait!"

She gave me the address and we said goodbye.

Cateline's enthusiasm made me smile, but my heart flipped with the anticipation of failure as well.

What if I let Cateline down? Would Cateline be shocked when she saw the real me?

Max stepped out of the bathroom in all his wet naked glory and distracted me from my worries about Cateline. I stared with my mouth agape as he walked toward me.

"Sammy?"

"Hm?" I rolled up onto my side and offered him the sexiest smile I could muster.

"I was asking you if there are any towels." Max laughed. "Didn't you hear me?"

"I don't think my ears work any more." I shook my head. "My eyes are taking up too much of my body's strength for anything else to work." I laughed at his expression.

"Anything?" He returned my seductive smile and stretched out on the bed beside me.

Soon every concern that weighed on my mind was obliterated by the sheer joy of Max.

After I took a quick shower, which involved my

standing on one foot at times, I crawled into bed. I hoped that I'd be able to fall right to sleep so that I would be refreshed in the morning.

Unfortunately, when I closed my eyes all of the concerns that Max had so skillfully whisked away from my mind began to return. I tried not to allow them to clutter my thoughts, but they insisted.

My stomach flipped and twisted. My heart pounded.

I didn't think I was ever going to reach a point of feeling confident that my books deserved so much attention. Many writers slaved away for decades before having any success, yet right off the presses my books were doing very well. Max insisted that it wasn't luck, but I was sure that it was.

What if, upon meeting me, Cateline realized that I was nothing more than a flash in the pan? Or worse, what if she thought I was a fraud?

I sighed and climbed out of bed. I didn't want my restlessness to wake Max.

I curled up on the window seat of the small window. For the first time I was glad that Poppy had given us a room on the third floor. The view of the street below was gorgeous, and it was now raining a bit.

The rain slid down the window in strange patterns. Maybe it was because of all of the webs and dirt that seemed to have collected along the unwashed surface. I couldn't look away from the intricate shapes that were created with just the subtlest obstacle in the raindrop's way.

Life unfolded like that for me. For a long time everything was in a straight line on the backdrop of a spotless surface, but now things were zigzagging and messy.

I was ready for the next step in my life, but was my life ready to keep up with me?

I drew my feet up onto the windowsill and closed my eyes. I imagined myself inside one of the chapters of my books.

Over time, the characters I'd created had become some of my closest friends. It was an odd truth that I wouldn't share with anyone, but I often found myself turning to them for advice and guidance. I didn't lose sight of the fact that they were fictional characters, but I did know that they were all aspects of myself in some way.

Sometimes it helped to imagine a conversation with one of them. Each and every one of them would have looked me in the eye and told me to be proud, to lead with my heart, not my fear.

I took a deep breath and focused on my body. One breath at a time I was able to settle my nerves.

Once I was feeling better, I returned to the bed and curled close to Max. He was my rock, there was no question of that, but I was strong enough to handle this. I just had to allow myself to be me.

CHAPTER 7

When I woke up the next morning, the bed beside me was empty. I sat up to look for Max and spotted a note on the bedside table.

Went for breakfast, be hungry.

I smiled and set the note back down.

I decided to select what I'd wear to the meeting.

I dug through my suitcase for a fresh pair of panties and a bra. I found the bra, but no matter how far I dug, I didn't find any panties—not a single pair. In desperation I dumped out the entire suitcase on the floor. I picked up every piece of clothing, but there was no underwear anywhere.

My heart began to speed up. How was that possible? Maybe I put them in another suitcase?

I sorted through all of the suitcases—even Max's—and found nothing.

All of a sudden it hit me that I'd packed another small bag at the last minute. It had all of my underwear as well as a few new pieces of lingerie. This bag was missing.

I grabbed my phone and tried to call the airline. I couldn't get through. I opened my computer to search for nearby stores to see if they were open. None of them appeared to be.

I was in full panic mode when the door of the room opened and Max stepped in with a brown paper bag.

"Sammy, why are your clothes everywhere?" Max stood at the entrance of the room and looked at the scattered clothes all over the bed, floor, and even the lamp.

"Max, the airport must have lost one of my bags! That's the only explanation! There's no way that I would have forgotten to pack underwear." I shook my head and put my hands on my hips. "How am I supposed to meet Cateline with no underpants?"

"Well, we could try to see if any stores are open—"

"I already have!" I pointed to my open laptop. "There's nothing open this early nearby."

"You don't have to wear underpants." He stepped into the room and closed the door. He set the brown paper bag down on the table beside the bed.

"Max, there is no way I can go to what's probably the most important meeting of my life without any underwear on."

"I go without underwear all the time." He shrugged.

"Women are different, Max! Wait, when do you go without underwear?"

Max frowned. "You know—now and then."

"Like when? At the movies? Were you going commando when we went to the park the other day?"

"Sammy."

"You're right, that's not important now. What is important is that I have nothing to cover my rear end with and I have to be at this meeting in less than an hour. Max, what am I going to do?"

He walked over to me and hugged me. "First, you have to calm down."

"Calm down?" I stared at him. "Did you not just hear me? This is a disaster!"

"Hold on a second. I have a very special gift for you."

"Max, not now." I shook my head. I was on the edge of a meltdown that I really didn't want Max to witness.

"I think you're going to like this. It's something I've never given to any other woman, and to be honest, something I never thought I would."

Despite the way my heart raced, his words made me curious. I looked over at him.

"What is it?"

"You have to close your eyes."

"Max! I don't have time for games."

"Sammy!" He pointed a finger at me. "If you want to know what it is, you have to close your eyes."

I stared at him with disbelief. I could see the crease in his forehead and the squint of the curve of his eyes. He was enjoying this.

"Fine." I closed my eyes.

"Now, Sammy, I'm giving you this because I love you, and over time we will learn to share all things." He placed something soft in my hands.

I opened my eyes to see a freshly folded pair of his underwear in my hands.

"What?" I met his eyes.

"You said you needed underwear." He smiled.

"But these are yours."

"Don't look so disgusted." He laughed. "They're brand new. I bought them for the trip."

"No, it isn't that. I'm sorry Max, of course I'd wear your underwear, any underwear—even old sweaty underwear." I winced. "Okay, maybe not sweaty."

Max tightened his lips to hold back laughter.

"It's not funny, Max! I can't wear men's underwear!"

"Why not?" Max's eyes widened. "It's not like Superman. If you put on the underwear I promise you won't magically turn into a man, or a superhero."

The image of me ducking into a phone booth to change into his underwear and emerging moments later as a bearded man did force a giggle from my throat.

"Okay, okay. You're right. But do you think they'll fit?" I stretched the waistband.

"They'll be fine." He kissed my cheek. "And thinking of you wearing them all day is kind of hot actually." He cleared his throat. "Maybe we should do this more often."

"Max, I'll do just about anything for you, but cross-dressing isn't one of them."

"What is? Maybe skinny-dipping? I hear the French like to go topless at the beach—"

"Max! I can't even think about that right now." I sighed.

"Okay, I know you're stressed." He hugged me again. "Why don't you get dressed and I'll set us up with breakfast on the balcony, okay? I got chocolate crepes!"

"Chocolate for breakfast? Max."

"You promised on the plane, remember? We'll be doing a lot of walking later. Trust me. You can handle a chocolate crepe."

I pouted but I didn't argue. I was more concerned about what I would wear to the meeting.

CHAPTER 8

As I sorted through my clothing options, all of my old insecurities rose to the surface.

The mirror was beautiful. I was sure it was antique, with a gold frame and an intricate design. But my reflection was another story. I tried a few things on but nothing looked nice. Most were either too tight or too baggy. I couldn't find that perfect balance.

Max poked his head in from the balcony just as I tugged on another dress that I could already tell was snug.

"You're not dressed yet?"

I smoothed the taut material over my hips and blinked back tears. I pulled the dress off and tossed it on the floor.

"Sammy, what was wrong with that? You look amazing in it. It's one of my favorites. The color brings out your eyes." Max walked over to me.

I stood in front of the mirror in nothing but my bra and Max's underwear.

"It's too tight."

"It is not. It shows off your figure perfectly."

I shook my head. "I don't want to look ridiculous."

"Sammy, don't you see how beautiful you are?" Max stared at my reflection in the ornate mirror. He reached out and brushed his hands along my shoulders and down my arms. "Every day I'm grateful that you agreed to marry me. I can't wait to open my eyes in the morning, just to see your face. That is not something that is ever going to change, no matter where we are or what happens in life. I just hope that you're able to see your own beauty as clearly as I do." He leaned close and kissed the side of my neck. "You own the world, Sammy, remember? You've created an entire career for yourself, and you're about to turn a success into a *wild* success. It's time you gave yourself credit for that."

"Oh, Max, I just got lucky." I tilted my neck toward his kiss. "I got lucky because I found an amazing man like you, and I got lucky because the right person read my book."

"No, Sammy. You worked hard to get to a point where you felt confident enough to try a relationship with me. You worked even harder to build your talent and confidence as a writer. *You* created this success. It wasn't luck. We're here together, with nothing to keep us apart, because you did this." He wrapped his arms around me and smiled. "Now go to that meeting and blow Cateline out of the water with your charming, funny, talented nature."

"Are you sure you shouldn't come with me?" I turned

in his arms and looked into his eyes.

"I could I suppose, but you don't need me to." He winked at me. "You've got this, babe. You've just got to remember to believe in yourself."

"Thanks, Max." As my lips met his, my entire body began to calm. My heart rate slowed, the heat in my cheeks faded to a subtle throb, and the twist in my stomach eased. By the time we broke the kiss, I felt grounded again.

"Get dressed and come eat." He met my eyes. "I don't want to have my first breakfast in Paris alone."

"Alright, I will." I smiled.

After Max left the room I picked up my favorite dress. I pulled it on and tugged it down over my hips. I didn't worry about what was rounder than it should have been, or what was flatter than I'd like. I looked at my reflection in the mirror and smiled at it.

"And thank you too, Sammy—for being brave enough to try."

After a quick comb and style of my hair and just a touch of make-up I headed out on to the balcony to join Max. The crepes looked amazing and tasted even better. I tried to eat around the chocolate but Max scooped up the gooey piece on his fork and held it in front of my lips.

"Trust me, you're going to need your strength."

"Oh?" I took the bite and savored the taste. "What do you have in mind?"

"I'll meet you after the meeting and we'll go

exploring. Okay?"

"Sounds good. I can't wait." I kissed his cheek.

I checked my make-up and hair very fast in the mirror and then raced out the door to my meeting.

It wasn't until I was several steps down the sidewalk that I realized wearing Max's underwear came with a real problem. A creeping up and getting stuck problem. I wiggled my bottom a few times in an attempt to set the bunch free, but that only made things worse. I lifted one foot high and then the other. That resulted in Max's underwear turning into a thong.

There were many people on the street. I couldn't discreetly tug or loosen.

In a last-ditch effort to free the underwear, I dropped my purse on the ground. Then I went into a full squat to pick it up. Finally the material slid back into its proper place, but the relief was accompanied by quite a few whistles and even a small amount of applause.

I looked over my shoulder to see that all of my wiggles and movements had slid my dress up along my hips to the point that when I squatted, my rear end was in full view of every person behind me on the street. I tugged it down fast and clenched my cheeks so tight that the underwear slid right back into the place it did not belong.

I hurried the rest of the way to the bookstore with my cheeks still clenched. I decided I'd rather have underwear tucked in the wrong places than my dress up around my hips.

CHAPTER 9

The bookstore was a bit smaller than I'd expected. It had two tall windows on either side of the door. The windows were filled with a variety of books on display. I noticed that there were several copies of my book included in the display.

A little thrill traveled up my spine at the thought of my book being promoted in a foreign country.

I tugged open the door and stepped inside. With a quick sweep I ran my hand over the curve of my bottom and tried to hide the out-of-place underwear.

The inside of the store was much roomier, with lots of comfortable places to curl up with a book.

I looked around and didn't see any sign of Cateline. I checked my phone to make sure that she hadn't called to change the meeting time. At that moment I received a text.

I'll be right there.

I texted back.

I'm here, but no rush.

I looked around the store one more time. It didn't

seem like anyone else was there. It struck me as odd that she would leave the door unlocked and the store unattended, but I assumed things might be a bit different in France.

I took advantage of my alone time and tried to force Max's underpants back into the right place. I had just dug them out, when a door to the back room swung open. A petite slender woman walked toward me with a smile so big that it seemed to consume her entire face.

"Hello! Samantha! It's so nice to finally meet you."

I smiled in return and was careful to offer the hand that I hadn't been using to fish for underwear with. "It's wonderful to meet you as well, Cateline."

I did my best to hide the surprise in my voice. I'd been expecting a woman with some girth, or at least someone who wouldn't be able to fit into a size zero, but this woman was one hundred pounds at best. She was shorter than me, and her features were small as well. She was what I would describe in one of my books as delicate.

"I'm sorry for the delay. I saw you come in on the security camera but I was just finishing up inventory."

Her words made my eyes widen. Camera? Had my underwear rescue been broadcasted to her in the back room? If it had, she didn't mention it.

"So how are you enjoying Paris so far?"

"To be honest, I haven't seen much of it." At least, not as much as Paris had seen of me, I thought. "But I can't wait to see all of the sights."

"You're going to love it. I tried to space your schedule so that you would have plenty of time for sightseeing. Also, I'd like to provide you with some transportation while you are here."

"Oh, that's too much, we can take care of that."

"Nonsense, I can't have my star writer getting lost or abducted by roaming bandits."

"No, that wouldn't be good." I laughed. I decided that I liked Cateline and her good sense of humor.

"Here is your schedule so we can get that out of the way. I also listed a few places you might like to see and some restaurants with a delicious menu." She quirked an eyebrow and smiled. "I see that you already tried some chocolate crepes. They're the best, aren't they?"

"How did you know?" I looked from her to the neckline of my dress. Splattered across the top of my breasts were a few drops of chocolate. "Oh no!" My cheeks grew hot.

"Oh, please don't worry." Cateline handed me a tissue from a box on the counter. "You're not the only one that gets chocolate on them, trust me."

I accepted the tissue and wiped at the chocolate. "I'm so sorry, you must think that I'm horrible."

"Horrible?" Cateline tilted her head to the side. "Why?"

"I mean, I shouldn't be eating things like that."

"If you fly all the way to France and don't try the amazing cuisine, *then* I think you're horrible." She grinned.

"Please, sit with me for a moment. I'd love to chat—to get to know you a little better."

I nodded and tossed the napkin into the trash can. I still had chocolate smeared across my skin but I did my best not to focus on it.

"Sure, that'd be great. Fire away. I'm happy to answer any questions." I gulped and tried to calm my nerves, which seemed to be flaring up again all of the sudden.

"Your words have such a powerful influence. Why do you think that is?" Cateline sat down across from where I'd seated myself on a fluffy green couch.

"I don't know if I could say that they're powerful."

"Ah, modesty. But you must know how influential your books have been, otherwise your sales wouldn't be so high—and you wouldn't be here."

"I guess I know in a way. I'm just not sure why they're so powerful. I'm honest and the words just come to me. In a lot of ways, I write what I need to hear myself."

"Raw and wise—I love it. I find that your message really speaks to me, because honestly, I'm always second-guessing how I look. It's sad to think that appearance has become so tied to self-worth."

CHAPTER 10

I was stunned that a woman like Cateline would even question her looks. I didn't see a single flaw. "That's true. I just feel that women all over the world are put under this undue pressure to meet a certain standard, and honestly, I don't even know what purpose it serves."

"Neither do I! When I put my make-up on in the morning, sometimes I stop and ask myself, who am I wearing this for? Now and then, the answer is for me, because I see nothing wrong with accentuating one's looks. But most of the time it's to look acceptable to my customers or people I meet throughout the day."

"I think many women feel that way—as if they have to look a certain way in order to even be accepted by society," I said.

"I hope that your book's message can change that."

"To be honest, Cateline—if they help one woman look into the mirror and feel proud, then I'll be happy."

"But of course it's not just about physical beauty. It's about the journey and challenging yourself again and again so that you can get to the core of who you are and what you want. Isn't it?"

"Oh, yes." I nodded. "My life has changed so much in just a short span of time, all because I traded fear for growth. I try to face whatever hardship I encounter with an ounce of curiosity. Why is this happening? Where will it lead me?" I thought about the clothes scattered all over the room that morning. "Of course, sometimes I still slip into old habits."

"Don't we all?" Cateline laughed and shook her head.

"Can I ask you a question, Cateline?"

"Sure."

"What made you pick up my book and read it?"

"I'd heard about it from a friend of mine. She told me that there was a book I just had to read and that she felt all women should read. So of course I had to try it, and once I did, I was blown away. That's when I knew you'd be perfect for this tour. You'll start with my bookstore and move on throughout France to other stores. They're all owned by women who want to support female writers who have an inspiring or influential message. I'd say that you fit that bill perfectly. Wouldn't you?"

I smiled. "I like to think so. I'm just so happy to be here."

"I'm happy to have you Samantha. But I don't want to stop you from getting a little sightseeing done. So why don't you take the rest of the day and share it with your husband? If you'd like, we could all meet for dinner tonight—with the friend that I told you about."

"I'd love that, thank you."

"Great, I'll call you with a time and place. Oh, and don't forget this." She handed me a business card. "This is Jean-Paul. He's a friend of mine that runs a car service. Anywhere you are in Paris—if you'd like a ride, just call him and one of his drivers will pick you up. Alright?"

"Thank you so much." I took the card and then stood up.

"It was a pleasure to meet you, Samantha."

"And you as well."

I walked out of the bookstore with Max's underwear in the wrong place yet again and the business card tucked into my purse. I found Max waiting outside.

"I thought you might be done by now." He raised an eyebrow as he looked at the chocolate smeared across my chest. "What were you two doing in there?"

"Ha, ha. You could have told me I dripped chocolate on my chest!"

"Maybe I was saving it for a snack later." He winked.

"Oh, gross, Max." I swatted his shoulder.

"I'm kidding. I honestly didn't notice. How did it go?"

"It went great. We have our own car service we can call if we need it and Cateline wants us to meet for dinner tonight. I hope that doesn't throw a wrench into any of your plans."

"Not at all." He shook his head. "It's perfect." He held out his arm to me. "Shall we."

"Uh, just a minute." I wiggled my bottom.

"Hm?" He grinned. "Are we dancing?"

"We're trying to get your undies in the right place."

"Oh my, sounds like we'll just have to go shopping." He wiggled his eyebrows. "Do I get to pick?"

"That sounds like a dangerous idea."

"It's only as dangerous as you let it be."

"Hm. Maybe I should do the picking."

"Where's your sense of adventure, Sammy?"

"It got lost with my panties!" I laughed.

Max slid his arm around my waist and we walked down the sidewalk.

"Should we call for Cateline's car service?"

"Yes, but let's stop in here real quick first." He pointed to a small boutique.

We ducked inside. The shop was eclectic, with lots of little unique items. There was a small assortment of underpants to choose from. Max picked up a pair of tiny black lacy panties.

"Perfect!"

"Only if you're wearing them."

"What?" Max's face drained of color.

"Well, it only seems fair, since I've been wearing yours all day." I smiled.

"Okay, okay, you can pick your own underwear." He sighed.

I found a few plain ones in my size and took them to the register. I paused when I saw the clerk behind the counter was a young man. Could I really endure buying underpants in front of him? I looked over at Max, who seemed to be mesmerized by a set of fuzzy dice.

"Max, I have to use the restroom. Can you check out for me?" I handed him the underwear before he could answer.

Max walked up to the register. I watched from the corner of the store as the clerk picked up each pair of underpants, then looked at Max. When he got to the last one he sighed.

"Sir, I think we have a problem here."

"What is it?" Max frowned.

I tried not to giggle.

"Well, let's forget that you clearly do not have very good taste, and talk instead about the fact that these are not your size. You're going to be back tomorrow to return them. Go try them on if you don't believe me."

Max looked over his shoulder. I knew he was looking for me.

I hid behind a stack of chairs.

"They're not for me, they're for my wife."

"Oh, sure, of course." The clerk rolled his eyes. "Are you sure you don't want to try them on?"

"No. Thank you. They're for my wife. Sammy."

"Sam? Is that your wife?" The man nodded with a smile behind the counter. "Don't worry sir, I understand." He bagged up the underwear and scanned the credit card.

When Max walked toward the door his cheeks were red. He caught sight of me hidden behind the chairs.

"That wasn't very nice of you." He quirked an eyebrow and held out his hand to me. "You owe me."

"I'm sure that we can settle up somehow." I grinned and snatched the bag from him. "Besides, you might have to borrow these one day. It wouldn't have killed you to try them on."

"It might have." He grimaced. "There's a restroom around the corner if you want to change, and I can call the driver while you're doing that."

"That sounds like the best idea I've heard all day! I love your underwear, Max—when you're wearing it."

"I'll keep that in mind."

CHAPTER 11

It was a relief to change out of Max's underwear. I was excited about where we might be going and content to let him surprise me.

As I walked toward the corner where Max and the car were waiting, it struck me that I was really in Paris. I was living out one of my dreams, and the best part was, I got to share it all with the love of my life.

I grinned widely as Max opened the door for me and we settled into the back seat.

"Better?" He plucked at the hem of my skirt as if he might peek.

"Stop that." I laughed. "Much better."

"I'll try not to be offended."

The traffic was as bad as I'd ever seen in any city, but Max and I utilized the time to discuss my meeting with Cateline.

When the car rolled to a stop, I looked out the window to see where we were.

"Oh, Max—the Eiffel Tower!" I could barely stay in

my seat when I saw it looming before us. I was so excited to get closer.

"I thought we could use a little exercise." He grinned and held out my sneakers. "We can walk the stairs as far as we'd like and then there's also an elevator if we need it."

"This is just what I need, Max. Thanks so much."

"Hey, I'm just looking out for my boss." He winked at me.

"Max, I'm not your boss."

"Oh yes, you are." He stepped out of the car.

I joined him from the other side. "Max, we're a team."

"Maybe, but you're the one who keeps the cash flowing, baby. I'm the one that oils the gears."

"Well, fine. If I'm the boss, then I guess you're my master."

"Wait a minute, I like the sound of that." Max laughed out loud.

"What? Master Max?" I winked at him.

"Hm, when you say it like that my imagination is going a bit wild." He laughed.

"Well, you're the webmaster, right? Without you I wouldn't be on the World Wide Web." I winked at him again.

"With ancient terms like that, I'd tend to agree with you. Let's go, boss, we've got a sight to see."

"Yes, master, whatever you say."

"That's actually really unnerving."

"Good to know." I grinned.

As we joined the long line at the Eiffel Tower I curled my hand around his. Even though there were many ways I enjoyed touching Max, holding his hand was still my favorite. There was something about the softness of his palm, the tickle of his fingertips, and the sensation of being held that always settled my mind.

We made it to the entrance and took the time to learn a bit about the Eiffel Tower's history. Then we boarded one of the elevators. I didn't realize the mistake we made until the elevator started to move. Instead of choosing one that was enclosed we had boarded the elevator that was open-air.

"Oh, Max, I don't know if I'm okay with this." I tightened my grip on his hand.

"Oh, this is nothing. Wait until we get to the top. I've arranged to bungee jump from the top of the Eiffel Tower. I thought you'd love it."

I gasped and looked into his eyes. "You didn't?"

The glimmer in his gaze gave him away. "I didn't. But this will be fine. Trust me. Just look at what we can see."

I did look, and he was right. The view was well worth the small dose of fear that accompanied it.

Once we reached the second floor, we left the elevator behind and joined several other people on the stairs.

"Isn't this great?" Max looked over at me. "Did you

ever think we'd be doing this?"

I smiled. If I were honest, I'd have to say yes. I had spent a lot of time using my imagination about the things I would do with Max if he ever returned my affection.

"I'm glad we're here."

"Me too." He kissed my forehead. "None of this would be happening without you, Sammy. You should be very proud."

His words were meant to be kind, but they tweaked a nerve within me.

I still didn't know how to accept that I was successful. I think a small part of me was still waiting for everything to fall apart. Life couldn't be this easy, could it? Life couldn't be this good, without the payment of some kind of price, right?

As I recognized that I still carried this belief deep within me, I could clearly see that it was an area I needed to work on. I decided to try to incorporate it into my next book.

By the time we headed back down the stairs my legs burned with the effort. It was easy to notice that I'd slacked off on my exercise regimen. My body was getting out of shape, and my stamina had diminished.

"You doing okay?" Max gave my back a light pat.

I wondered if he felt all of the sweat gathered there. It was good that I had sneakers on, but the dress was still snug and constrictive.

"Just a little disappointed at how much I've let my

exercise go."

"Don't worry about that, Sammy. Soon we'll be running on the beach."

A sudden, horrifying image of me running down the beach topless with my breasts flopping and slapping made me so dizzy that I had to grab Max's arm to get down the last few steps. Even the idea of running in a bikini was a bit much, but topless? I really needed to research this whole topless at the beach idea that they had going on here.

"I'm looking forward to being in the water again." I cleared my throat and avoided the topless topic.

"Why don't we head back for a rest before dinner?"

"Perfect." I gave him a quick kiss on the lips and thought about the relief I'd feel getting out of my dress.

CHAPTER 12

When we arrived at the bed and breakfast Poppy was waiting for us. She had a bronzed Maltese tucked under her arm.

"I thought you might like some food to nibble on out on the patio. I've prepared a few things for you." She smiled.

I was tired, but I was also very hungry. "Thank you, we'd love that."

She led us out to the patio, which was filled with even more animal statues. There were even a few birds, a rabbit, and a squirrel. Max and I exchanged a look across the table as we sat down. The patio overlooked a small patch of untended grass. A ceiling fan wobbled in a slow circle above our heads.

Poppy returned with a platter of cheese and fruit as well as some bread.

"I hope this will be enough. There's more if you need it, just ask." She set two wine glasses down on the table, one in front of each of us. "I took the liberty of opening my favorite wine for you to sample."

"Oh, I don't know, is it too early for wine?" I looked across the table at Max.

"Is it ever too early for wine?" Max grinned. "Not in Paris."

"Listen to your husband, he knows!" Poppy laughed and went back into the house to retrieve the bottle of wine.

"This bed and breakfast may not be what I'd imagined, but Poppy has certainly been a wonderful host."

"Yes, and there may not be any other guests, but at least we have plenty of animals to keep us company." Max chuckled.

Poppy returned and filled our glasses to the very top.

"Now I'll leave you two alone. I'm sure you have much to discuss." Poppy hurried away.

Max picked up his glass and held it out to me.

"To Paris."

"To Paris." I clinked my glass with his.

We each took a sip of the wine. I expected it to be a rather cheap or offbeat flavor, as Poppy seemed to dance to her own beat, but it was the most delicious wine I'd ever tasted.

"Wow!" I looked over the rim of my glass at Max.

"I know. It's great." He took a long swallow. "I don't think I've ever tasted better. We should find out what it is. Maybe we can take a few bottles home with us."

"Max, do you realize that we're not going to be home

for a year?" My eyes widened.

"Oh, I guess we could just order some."

"No, that's not what I mean. I just can't quite wrap my head around the fact that we are going to be traveling for that long. It's amazing, isn't it?"

"Yes, it is. I guess it hasn't really set in with me yet either. Where are we headed next?"

"Italy, I think. I have to check with Cateline to be sure."

"Ah, Italy, the country of romance."

"Really? I thought that was France?"

"Sure France is romantic, but Italy—Italy is for lovers."

"Why do you think that?" I picked up a piece of cheese.

"In France the food is delicious, but it's all about presentation. In Italy, the food is real. It's rich, it's flavorful, and served in copious amounts. Entertainment is designed to savor each other rather than separate each other."

I smiled as I listened to his words. "The way you describe it makes me want to be there right this second."

"Good thing we don't have too long to wait."

After we finished our meal, I went back in to try to figure out what to wear to dinner.

Then I sat down at my computer. While I typed away, Max lounged on the bed with a book. This was the first time since I'd arrived in France that I'd actually sat down to work. The first few paragraphs flew right out of my fingers, but then I hit a block. There was an unease within me that I just couldn't shake. I decided to try to write it out.

I opened a new document and just wrote what was on my mind. As the words formed on the page, I found that most of my concern stemmed from insecurity. Here I was in a new country, with people who'd never met me. I was surrounded by the beauty of Paris as well as the beautiful people of Paris. Rather than fully embracing that beauty, I'd tried to tuck myself away, as I felt I didn't fit. I could see the old habits that were rearing their ugly head.

I took a deep breath and tried to focus on my confidence level. As I returned to the book, I found that I could write a few more paragraphs, but it was nothing like what I truly wanted to say. My words were stilted and the imagery just wasn't there. Even with a big glass of wine in me, I couldn't relax.

"You okay, Sammy?" Max looked over at me from the bed.

"I guess. I'm having a little trouble getting into the groove."

"Well, don't worry about it. We have dinner tonight, then tomorrow we can explore in the morning and spend the afternoon hard at work. I have some tweaks I need to do to the website anyway. Then we have the reading."

"I guess you're right. Maybe I'm just putting too much pressure on myself to produce."

"You know that always slows you down." Max stood up and walked over to me. He began to rub my shoulders. I melted beneath his touch. It transported me to a peaceful state of mind.

"I know, Max, but this isn't a vacation. It's work."

"But work doesn't always have to be hard." Max smiled and brushed his lips along my cheek. "It can be wonderful."

Something about the way he purred the word made me turn so that I could kiss him. He stood me up from the chair and spun me against his chest. I shivered with anticipation as he guided me toward the bed.

"It's not a honeymoon either." I managed to speak the words between kisses.

"Everyday is a honeymoon with you, Sammy." He sat down on the edge of the bed and then tugged me down beside him.

I decided I had no interest in resisting. As I was about to disrobe I noticed a tiny cat curled up on the bookshelf. I was startled by it, as I didn't think that there were any animal statues in our room.

"Max, it's watching us."

"Huh?" Max tried to draw my lips back to his.

"Max, there's a cat statue."

"So what?" He sighed.

"It's creepy."

"Only if you look at it." He turned my face back to his and kissed me again.

I pulled away and shook my head. "No, I'm sorry. I can't. I feel like it's staring at me."

"Sammy, it's a statue, how can it be staring at you?"

"Please, Max."

"Okay, fine. I'll get rid of it, but don't you move from that bed, understand?" He met my eyes with a stern look.

I smiled. "I have no intention of moving." I stretched out on the bed in what I thought was a sexy pose but might, in fact, have been all hips and elbows jutted at awkward angles.

Max hurried over to the bookshelf and looked up at the cat. "Wow, that's an amazing statue." He had to stand on his toes to reach it.

As he grabbed it, I heard a grunt, followed by a loud hissing noise.

"Max? What are you doing?" I sat up just in time to get smacked in the face by the furry side of a cat. It landed on the bed and than scurried for the door. Max gasped and jerked the door open to let it out. Then he slammed the door closed. He turned to look at me with wide eyes and a pale face.

"I thought you said it was a statue!"

"I thought it was." I picked some black fur out of my mouth.

"Are you okay?" He walked back over to the bed.

"I'm fine." I laughed. "Maybe it was a sign that I need to get back to work."

"Oh, it was a sign alright." Max sprawled out on the

bed and then pulled me down next to me. "That we should stay in bed where it's safe." His kisses along my neck convinced me that he was right.

CHAPTER 13

When I woke up from our afternoon romp and nap, I realized that I'd not set an alarm. I grabbed my phone and saw that it was only a half hour before the time we were due to meet Cateline and her friend at the restaurant.

"Max! Max! We're going to be late!" I tried to jump out of bed but the blanket was tangled around me and tucked under Max. I landed in a pile on the floor, still rolled up in the blanket.

"Sammy?" Max sat up sleepily. "What are you doing down there?" He wiped at his eyes.

"Get me out of this!" I wiggled around, much like a fish might flop around on a dock. The more I tried to unwind from the blanket the more stuck I seemed to become.

Max laughed and grabbed one end of the blanket. He unrolled me with one hard tug.

"We have to go, we're going to be late, get dressed."

"Okay, it's going to be fine, Sammy. Try not to worry." He reached for me but I was too focused on getting dressed.

"It's not going to be okay if we're late. I don't want to make a bad impression. Max! Please, just get dressed."

"Okay, okay." He got out of bed and sorted through the closet for the suit he'd hung up.

By the time we met the car outside, we had only ten minutes to spare.

"Do you think we'll make it?"

Max put his hand over mine and smiled. "I know we will."

Max's ability to stay calm in stressful situations always amazed me, especially when he was in those situations with me.

We arrived right on time at the restaurant. My heart pounded from the panic of the race to get there. I smoothed my hair and took a deep breath.

Max led me into the restaurant, which was quite crowded. I spotted Cateline not far from the entrance. She was already seated, along with another woman who had thick, dark, curly hair and was closer in size to me than petite Cateline. She and Cateline leaned close as they talked.

"There they are, Max."

"Oh, good, I'm starving."

The hostess led us toward the table. As soon as we neared it the other woman stood up so fast that she knocked into the table. The water glasses trembled but did not fall over.

"Samantha! I can't believe it's you." She grinned and held out her hand to me. "My name is Agnes DuBois. I'm a huge fan—probably your biggest fan. I can't believe I'm meeting you in person!" She squeaked out her final words and gave the hand I offered her a firm squeeze.

"It's nice to meet you." I was a little startled by how excited she was and also completely flattered. "This is my husband, Max."

"It's a pleasure to meet you, Max." She shook his hand as well.

Once we were all seated at the table, Agnes began to gush.

"When I heard about the book tour that Cateline was interested in starting, I knew you had to be part of it. I have to say that your book has been the most powerful book I've ever read."

"Oh, I don't know about that, but I'm glad that you liked it. I'm sorry we're a little late."

"Not at all, you're right on time. We got here a little early so I could talk Agnes' ear off about the tour. Please sit." Cateline smiled at Max. "So you're the famous husband, Max."

"Famous?" He raised an eyebrow and pulled out a chair for me.

"I might brag about you now and then." I grinned at him.

He smiled in return and sat down beside me.

"Well, then I guess we're even because I sure do brag

about my lovely wife."

"How could you not?" Agnes piped up.

The waitress approached the table to take our orders. I selected something I was familiar with, as I didn't want to risk a food disaster in front of Agnes and Cateline. Max followed suit, and we both ordered wine.

"So, Samantha, what have you seen so far in Paris?" Cateline picked up her own glass of wine.

"Max took me to see the Eiffel Tower. It was quite an experience."

"It always is." Agnes nodded. "I've gone a dozen times but I'm still awed by it. There's one place you simply must go, though, as I think you'll really enjoy it." She pulled out a pen and jotted down the address on a napkin, then handed it to me. "Trust me, it's one place that you don't want to miss."

"Thank you." I tucked the napkin safely into my purse.

"Samantha, before our food arrives why don't we talk about the reading tomorrow night?" Cateline picked up her phone and tapped the screen. "I just want to make sure it goes smoothly, as it is the opening of the tour."

"Oh, yes, of course." I nodded.

"You will do your reading and then we'll have an autograph session after. Does that sound okay to you?"

"Absolutely. I'm just so grateful for this opportunity."

"We're glad to have you. As you can see, my friend Agnes is just a small example of the amount of impact that you've had on your readers. In fact, we expect to have a full house tomorrow."

I bit into my bottom lip to prevent a wince. I had done a few small readings but this wasn't just a reading. This was the launch of a book tour, and I was nervous.

"I just have to ask—I'm dying to know Samantha— how is the next book coming along?" Agnes leaned close to me across the table.

I nearly choked on the sip of wine that filled my mouth.

"Uh, well, it's progressing."

"Oh, sure, it's probably about done, right? I mean, your readers are chomping at the bit to get to that next book. As soon as it's out, I'm sure it will fly off the shelves."

CHAPTER 14

I stared at Agnes with a mixture of pride and horror. I couldn't even imagine the next book being done. It was barely started and what was written was not exactly my best work. Luckily the food arrived before I had to lie to cover up how much I'd slacked off.

"Well, with the book tour and all, we've had to adjust our timeline a little." Max smiled to cover my apprehension.

"That's right, you're helping Samantha out?" Cateline nodded to the waitress as she received her food. "That must be so lovely to work together. Now what is it that you do, Max?"

"He's my master." I blurted the words out as my plate was placed in front of me. The waitress gave me an odd look and hurried off. Agnes and Cateline looked at one another and then back at me.

Only then did I realize what I'd said.

Max appeared to be covering his mouth with a napkin to hide his laughter.

"Webmaster! Oh, my." I shook my head and blushed.

"I mean, he runs my website for me and takes care of all the technical aspects of my work. Without him, I wouldn't be able to do any of this."

Agnes giggled. "Oh, that kind of master. That makes sense."

"Well, no matter what kind of master he is to you, I'm sure you both love working together. I don't know if I could do that with my husband. We'd probably murder each other," Cateline said.

"I think we work well together." Max glanced over at me.

"Oh, yes. Though sometimes he can be a little distracting." I shot a look over at Max as the toe of his shoe pushed against the smooth curve of my ankle.

"And she can nitpick the tiniest thing." Max quirked an eyebrow.

"Well, no matter. When that book comes out, I can't wait to read it."

I felt a surge of frustration. Here I was having a meal with two women who fully supported my writing and I couldn't even be bothered to get the next book ready to go. In the back of my mind I had promised myself that I would buckle down and get some work done before I headed off to Italy, and now I was paying for my lack of diligence.

I picked up my fork to take a bite of my food. As I stabbed the fork into a piece of meat, it slid through the gravy and right off my plate onto the white tablecloth.

"Oops, it looks like someone's dinner got away." Agnes laughed.

Max reached over with his napkin.

"Pesky meat. It never stays on my plate." He chuckled as he wrapped up the meat and set it aside.

I looked over at Max with a small smile of gratitude.

When I tried again I managed to get the meat into my mouth. Then I reached for my glass of wine to wash it down. When I lifted my arm, my elbow knocked into Max's silverware and sent it rolling off the table. I groaned and reached down to get it.

"No, let me. I'm just a little clumsy tonight. I'm so sorry." Max collected the silverware.

I realized that he had covered for me yet again.

"Don't worry, Max, we all get a little clumsy now and then," said Cateline. "Isn't that right, Samantha?" She raised her wineglass.

"I can toast to that!" I picked my glass up as well, but the base of the glass was stuck in the gravy left behind by the meat, so the tablecloth lifted up with it. I tried to yank it free, and the sudden gesture caused my entire plate of food to land in my lap.

"Oh, dear." Cateline pursed her lips. She set her glass of wine down on the table.

Agnes jumped up and tugged off her blazer.

Max grabbed the plate out of my lap and tried to hide the fact that he was using a napkin to scoop meat, gravy, and rice out of my lap.

I could only close my eyes and try not to scream.

"Here, Samantha, you can wear this. It's long enough, it should cover any stains." Agnes smiled.

I looked up at her. "Really? Thank you."

"Of course. We all make mistakes."

"Me, more than most, it seems." I sighed and shook my head. "Thanks, Max."

"That's what I'm here for." He piled the lap food onto my plate and gestured to the waitress. As the waitress took the plate Cateline leaned toward her.

"Please bring a fresh meal."

"Oh, no, that's okay, I'm fine." My stomach was in knots.

"I insist. It's important that you eat, Samantha. I find that a good bellyful of food always helps me sleep well, and I want you awake and perky at the reading."

I began to relax. I could see that these two women weren't there to judge me. They liked my book, and they were willing to accept the chaos that was me along with it. I ate my meal with careful movements.

After dinner we lingered outside the restaurant while we waited for the car service to return.

"Don't forget to check out that place I told you about. It's a garden and it's gorgeous."

"I've got it right here." I patted my purse and smiled. "Thank you both—for everything."

"Thank you." Agnes met my eyes. "I really mean that, Samantha. Being a woman of size in the fashion epicenter of the world hasn't exactly been easy for me. Your book has taught me to find my own beauty, and I don't even know how to express my gratitude for that."

"Never doubt your strength, Samantha." Cateline gave me a quick pat on the shoulder. "You are honest, you are in touch with yourself, and the people around you, and you know how to reach the hearts of others. That's a special talent, even without being a gifted writer."

"You are too kind." I hid the blush in my cheeks as I looked away.

The car pulled up to the curb.

"See you tomorrow night, Samantha. Please let me know if you have any trouble, okay?"

"Cateline, is there any certain way that you'd like me to dress?" I glanced down at the stain on my skirt. "I'm guessing less gravy."

"Less gravy would be good." Cateline laughed. "But other than that, please just wear what you feel comfortable in."

"Okay." I started to take off the blazer to return it to Agnes.

"Please, keep it. I have plenty more." She waved to me as she and Cateline walked away.

"Lovely people." Max nodded toward them.

"Yes—yes, they are." I smiled.

CHAPTER 15

Early the next morning Max and I set off for the address that Agnes had given me. The driver recognized it and headed straight for it. After a short drive the car slowed down. He dropped us off at a beautiful spindled gate. On the front of the gate a sign displayed the name of the garden.

"Here you are. Would you like me to wait?" The driver glanced into the back seat.

"No, it's fine, we can call when we're ready." I opened the door and walked toward the gate. Max followed after me after tipping the driver.

"This looks very interesting." He pushed opened the gate and we walked through.

On the other side were sprigs of purple flowers that seemed to blossom from the cracks of the pavement. There were several elevated gardens to see as we moved down the first path. Interspersed with the flowers were small statues. I didn't recognize the figures, but I did enjoy seeing them amidst the petals.

"This is very nice. I'm glad that Agnes suggested it."

Max pointed to a nest that was hidden in the low branches of a small tree. "It looks like there might be babies in there."

"Aw, baby birds?" I tried to peer through the branches. "Where? I can't see them."

"Right there." Max tried to point out the nest again.

I really wanted to see the tiny little creatures so I ducked my head under the low branch in an attempt to get a closer look. As I did, my shoulder bumped into something. It moved a little when I bumped into it. Then I heard a very strange sound. The sound reminded me of something, but I couldn't quite place what it was. I continued to look for the nest.

"Sammy! Get out of there!" Max's hands gripped my shoulders and he tugged.

"Max, stop, you're going to scare the babies." I stumbled back and all at once I recognized the sound. Bees! They were everywhere. I must have bumped into a hive.

I scrambled away from the tree in an attempt to escape the bees, but the buzzing sound followed me. I felt the burning sensation of bee stings on my face, shoulders, and arms. I started to panic, as everywhere I turned there were more bees that swarmed me.

Max pulled off his shirt and waved it at the bees. That only seemed to make them angry. When one of the bees stung the side of my neck I started to run. I ran as fast as I could down the path. The bees managed to keep up with me but not many were stinging. I hoped for shelter but there was only more garden.

Then I spotted a large fountain in the center of all of the garden paths. Without hesitation I launched myself into the fountain. It was just deep enough that I could completely submerge my body. I stayed under the cold murky water for some time. Max's hand slid under my arm and he pulled me up out of the water.

"No, the bees!" I tried to pull away.

"They're gone, Sammy, look. It's okay." I peeked over the side of the fountain. I didn't hear any buzzing or see any bees.

"Are you sure?"

Max helped me out of the fountain.

"Excuse me, that is not a swimming pool!" A woman in a green uniform marched up to me.

"I'm sorry, there were bees and—" I turned to face the woman.

She gasped when she saw my face.

"Come with me, I have some cream to treat those. Oh dear, you poor thing." She took my hand and led me to a small white building. I hadn't even seen it, as it was tucked behind some thick trees. She opened the door and I was greeted by a very sweet smell. The room was filled with flowers.

"I'm preparing for a wedding." She gestured to a rolling chair. "I'm not really supposed to do this, but I can't let you suffer. I've been stung by those nasty bees before."

My face throbbed with multiple bee stings. I blinked back tears, as the pain was intense, but it wasn't just the pain that upset me. It was the experience. Everything had been going well, and now everything was ruined. I had the reading that night, and now I was covered in bee stings. How was I going to be able to stand in front of a crowd like that?

"Thank you." Max spoke up as the woman pulled out a bottle of cream.

"Yes, thank you."

"It's the least I can do. I'm sorry that this has happened to you. We can't remove the bees as they are vital to the ecosystem, but they are very pesky too."

"I was trying to see a nest and bumped into the hive."

"Yes, nature has a way of being vengeful if disturbed."

"Are you sure that she doesn't need to go to a hospital?" Max frowned as the woman covered each sting with cream.

"Unless she starts to swell up, she should be fine. Have you ever had any allergic reaction to bee stings before?"

"No." I sighed as some of the burning subsided with the cooling effect of the cream.

"Then you should be fine. You can take this with you. Just reapply it whenever the stinging starts up. Alright?" She smiled and handed me the tube.

I took it from her and managed a smile in return. "I can't believe I was so stupid."

"You weren't stupid." Max shook his head. "It's my fault. I pointed out the nest."

"It's nobody's fault. It's just nature." The woman shrugged. "Some things just happen."

CHAPTER 16

Her words lingered with me as we waited for the car service to return. It occurred to me that we never would have been at the garden if it weren't for Agnes' suggestion. Somehow I'd been directed into this event. But why? Was I not supposed to do the reading that night? Was I not supposed to even be in Paris?

I was feeling rather sullen by the time we got back to the bed and breakfast. Max led me upstairs and tried to cheer me up with a glass of the delicious wine that Poppy offered to us. I sipped it and sighed.

"Sammy, I have to tell you something." Max met my eyes. His features were aligned in a very serious expression.

"What is it?" I braced myself for another blow.

"I thought you were the most beautiful woman I'd ever laid eyes on before."

"Before?" I frowned. "I know I'm a mess now."

"No. You look a million times sexier in polka dots." He winked.

I had to laugh. I didn't want to laugh. But I had to.

"Polka dots, huh? Do you think the people at the reading tonight will feel the same way?"

"Sammy, they're not going to be there to judge how you look. They're there because they love your work."

"I don't know, maybe I should cancel."

Max frowned. "I'll support whatever decision you make, but I think that showing up despite the difficulty that you've faced will have a much bigger impact."

I nodded a little and sat down with my glass of wine. I wanted to wallow, but talking to Max reminded me that I needed to bounce back. The bees didn't have anything against me, they didn't seek me out. It just happened. And now the only choice I had was how I'd deal with it.

I opened up my computer and decided to do a little writing about how to deal with difficult situations. In the past, my first instinct would be to turn to food or television to wipe away the frustration or stress.

I put together a short list of alternatives to that option: —meditation, focused breathing, a walk out in nature—preferably where there weren't any bees—a short nap to ease exhaustion.

As I read over the list I realized that I hadn't been employing any of my methods lately.

"Max, I think I'm going to do some meditation before we leave for the reading."

"You're going to go?" He smiled.

"Yes, you're right. It will be a good example. I just hope that Cateline will understand."

"She seems like the understanding type."

"True. I think a little meditation will help me get focused again."

"Alright, I'll take a walk. You enjoy." He smiled and kissed my cheek.

"Are you sure you don't want to join me?"

"Sweetheart, if we get into bed together, no meditation is going to get accomplished."

"Good point." I laughed.

Once Max was gone I settled into a lotus position in the middle of the bed. I took a deep breath and focused on its path through my nostrils down my windpipe and into my chest. Then I released.

I followed the same method several times until my body began to relax. My muscles relaxed and my body felt pounds lighter. Little aches and pains that I didn't even realize were there offered me some relief as they disappeared.

My face still ached a little from the stings, but I began to forget about the pain. Over and over I inhaled and exhaled. The room around me began to disappear.

I felt Zara surface within me. I felt her strength, her determination, and her courage. I recognized those things as not just a part of the fictional character that I'd birthed, but as a part of me. I'd drawn on my own experience, my own talents, to create Zara. She was as much me as I was.

That fierceness flooded through my veins. My lashes fluttered. An intense release of stress and attempts at control escaped me in a subtle sigh. Internally, I was wiped clean—to the point that my forehead relaxed, my lips parted, and my jaw loosened. The calming sensation spread down through the curves of my shoulders and erased the tension in my upper arms.

By the time I opened my eyes, my attitude was reborn. It didn't matter that I had bee stings, or that my next book still waited for my attention. I found the moment again, the moment I lived in, the moment in which I was surrounded by love and support.

I stood up and headed to the closet to search for what I'd wear to the reading.

"Sammy?" Max poked his head into the room. "Are you done?"

"Yes." I spun around and kissed him.

His eyes widened with surprise. "I think I like meditation."

"Me too." I grinned. "Let's head out early, okay? I don't want to spring the bee stings on Cateline at the last minute."

CHAPTER 17

When we walked into the bookstore Cateline was in the middle of arranging chairs. She looked up with a smile that faded when she saw my face.

"Oh, Samantha, what happened?"

"I got a little too in touch with nature." I laughed. "It's not as bad as it looks."

"What did this to you?" She walked over and looked at the welts.

"Bees."

"Oh, how horrible." She shook her head. "That doesn't sound like a very pleasant experience."

"No, it wasn't, but it's over now. I hope you don't mind, but I have to wear this white cream on the stings tonight to keep them from swelling."

"No, I don't mind. I just wish it hadn't happened."

"I did at first too, but to be honest, I got a lot of inspiration out of it."

She shook her head. "Only you could see the positive in such a painful experience."

"I had a little help from this guy." I smiled at Max.

"Can I give you a hand with the chairs?" Max walked toward the stack.

"That would be wonderful. We're going to need at least forty, so if you can make a bit of a semi-circle I think that would be perfect. What do you think, Samantha?"

"Forty?"

"Forty seated. We'll probably be closer to seventy-five total."

"Wow." I looked over the small space and imagined it packed with people. I imagined seventy-five pairs of eyes focused only on me. I wasn't sure that I was as brave as Zara after all. I drew a deep breath and reminded myself to be in the moment.

"Thanks for all of this, Cateline."

"No, thank you. All of these people are very likely to buy a copy of your book or many others on display. So it will be very good for the store. Not to mention that everyone is so excited to just get to know you a little bit. It's been so nice. I hate to share you with Isabella."

"Isabella?"

"Isabella is your contact for the tour in Italy. She'll be here for the question and answer session at the end of the week so that you can meet her."

"I'll look forward to meeting her. Do you think I should do a run-through of my reading before people arrive?"

"I think natural is always best. When you read to your

audience you don't want to sound rehearsed or you'll come off as unauthentic—don't you think?"

I nodded. "It makes sense."

My heart fluttered. *It's okay to be nervous, Sammy*, I assured myself. *Just don't let it stop you from succeeding.*

I closed my eyes for a moment and then walked over to help Max with the chairs. It didn't take us long to have them all set up. When we were finished Max sat down in one of the chairs.

"Go stand at the podium." He tilted his head toward a small podium with a microphone.

"Oh, Cateline didn't think I should rehearse."

"I just want to see you up there." Max smiled. "I'm so proud of you."

Inspired by his words, I made my way up to the podium.

I'd almost reached it when my foot got tangled in the cord of the microphone. I tried to shake it loose and reached with my opposite hand to rest my weight on the podium. What I didn't know—what I couldn't have possibly known—was that the podium was on wheels. When I leaned on it, it didn't just shift a little, it flew right out from under my grasp. With my foot still tangled in the cord and the microphone attached to the podium, I ended up in a very uncomfortable split on the floor.

"Ouch."

Max jumped up and ran over to me. "Oh my god, Sammy, are you alright?" He tucked his hands under my shoulders and lifted.

I stumbled to my feet, finally free of the cord, and looked at him. "I think so."

"I didn't know you could do that." He laughed.

"I don't think I can." I shook one leg and then the other to make sure that they were still attached. "Good thing I wore pants."

I started to walk toward the podium to put it back in place before Cateline noticed. I heard Max groan from behind me.

"What?" I looked over my shoulder and followed Max's eyes toward my bottom to see that my brand new French underpants were on display for the world to see— or at least seventy-five people. I looked at my watch. "There's no time to go back to the room and change."

"Well, you can have mine." Max raised an eyebrow.

I looked at his pleated trousers and grimaced. Underwear was one thing, but his pants would be long and bulky on me. It was not the professional image I wanted to project.

"I know!" I snapped my fingers. "Agnes' jacket! I brought it with me for luck. Can you get it for me?"

"Sure." Max walked over behind the counter where I'd dropped my purse and the blazer. He brought it back to me.

I slid my arms into the sleeves. They were a little long so I rolled them up. The blazer was just long enough to cover the tear in the seat of my pants.

"What do you think?" I grinned at Max.

"I think you look awesome as always. But are you comfortable?"

"Yes, actually. I'm feeling a breeze." I laughed. "That should keep me cool during the reading." I wiggled my bottom to show him how I could make a breeze, just as the door swung open.

A few people stepped in. Max moved in front of me in an attempt to shield my display but I heard a few giggles. Cateline walked out of the back room before I could explain myself. As I watched her try to hide a grin I remembered that she'd told me that there were cameras in the front of the store. My cheeks burned, but that might have been the bee stings.

"Oh, thanks so much. This looks great. Except, what's the podium doing over here?" Cateline pushed the podium back into place. "You'll want to be careful Samantha. It's on wheels, so it moves easily."

I could have been wrong, but I was fairly certain that she gulped back a laugh. I tugged the blazer down over my pants and smiled at the next batch of people who stepped in. Within about twenty minutes at least sixty people had arrived. The chairs were filled and people were also standing near the bookshelves.

"I guess we should get started." Cateline glanced at her watch, then at me. "Are you ready for this, Samantha?"

CHAPTER 18

In the moment, in the moment, I chanted in my mind.

"Yes, I am. In the moment." I winced as Cateline looked confused. "Sorry."

I made my way toward the podium. Cateline stepped up to it first to introduce me.

"Tonight we have a very special author with us. We're going to let her kick off our book tour, Worldwide Wonder Women, which as you all know is a tour designed to showcase female authors whose books are particularly inspiring.

"Tonight we have the author of the book *Becoming Zara* and her new series *B.I.G. Girls Club*—" She paused as applause interrupted her.

I couldn't help but smile.

"Yes, it is quite popular." Cateline laughed. "Samantha, I'll let you take it from here."

Bubbles and butterflies danced around in my stomach as I traded places with Cateline at the podium.

"Thank you all for being here tonight. I'm so glad to have the opportunity to share a little bit of my work with you. I'm going to read a passage from *Becoming Zara* where Zara is also standing in front of a room full of women, much like yourselves."

I felt the goosebumps up and down my arms as I realized the irony of this moment for myself, and I had to blink back a sudden tear at the emotion I was suddenly feeling as I looked out at the sea of faces looking up at me expectantly. I took a deep breath in.

"I hope that this connect with your hearts."

I didn't stop to think about whether my words were cheesy or longwinded.

I opened my copy of the book to the highlighted section that I was to read. I took a deep breath, and felt Zara's bravery rush through me.

Then I began to read. As I did, I tried to vocalize the emotions that I'd felt as I wrote it.

"I glanced around the brightly lit room, taking in the twenty or so women of various sizes and shapes, most of whom seemed to at least match my two hundred pounds—okay, maybe two hundred pounds on a good day. Peeling off the name tag sticker that I'd just filled out, I caught myself grinning as I patted it down on my jeans—right in the middle of my thigh, which I'd only recently started to appreciate. I stifled a laugh as my new shower ritual played in my mind. Soap up the squeegee thingy and lovingly talk to your body as you wash and caress it. Just that morning I'd told my thighs that they were an absolute thing of beauty and they—so graciously—rewarded me by sliding into my jeans with only a hint

of trouble. Turning my attention back to the ladies now seating themselves in the chairs set around the room in a circle, I could see their name tags over their hearts. Mary, Jane, Lucy, Maxine, Susan, Nicole…I glanced down again at my own name tag, giving it one last pat. Zara…warrior princess, I added in my head."

I continued to read through the next few pages, and as the last word hung in the air, the women in the audience were quiet. I looked up from the book and out to their faces as I wondered if I'd flopped. I noticed that several of the women nodded to one another. Some even dabbed at their eyes with a tissue. There were women of all shapes and sizes, of all ages and races.

They were there because they heard something in my words. They heard what it was like to be a woman— learning to love and accept herself.

As the applause began I barely noticed. My attention was focused on the notes being scribbled, the hands being held, and the words being whispered. I realized then that my words had an impact on a group of strangers. These weren't women who knew me, or even shared the same city as me. These were women that lived entirely different lives and yet they could relate to everything I'd just read.

Cateline nodded with a smile from the counter.

I continued, smiling at the women in front of me. "As you all know, we all write our own stories. I like to think of our bodies as being the keepers of that story. So when we look at something on our body and consider it a flaw, it's important to remember that flaw has a story and a purpose—a beauty all its own."

Another round of applause followed my words. I found Max where he stood in the back of the crowd. His small slow smile reminded me of the first time I knew I loved him. The pride in his eyes was clear.

I stepped away from the podium and headed toward him. Before I could reach him, a woman stood up and stepped in front of me. She reminded me of myself, with her nervous hands and her voluptuous waist.

"Samantha, I know this isn't the question and answer session, but I was just wondering if I could ask you a quick question."

Cateline shook her head but I ignored her. I wanted to be available to my readers.

"Sure, what is it?"

"I really love what Zara does—the shower ritual. When I do something like that, it works for me while I'm alone. But the moment I get out into the world with other people, I just want to cover up and hide. How do you get to a point where you're so comfortable and confident with your body that you don't feel that shame around other people?"

I stared into her anxious eyes. Her words hit home with me, because her description of how she felt was exactly how I felt about going to the beach with Max. Seeing my own insecurity reflected in this woman's eyes made me realize just how poorly I treated my own body by telling it it wasn't good enough for the beach. I felt sympathy for her—and for myself—because we were so programmed to believe that our bodies weren't perfect.

"I think it takes baby steps. We know in our heart that our bodies are beautiful just the way they are. But when we brace ourselves for the judgment of others, we worry. I've gone through different stages of progress in that regard. I hope that one day I'll be able to say to you that I'm one hundred percent comfortable stark naked in the middle of a crowd. But as of now, I still struggle with that too. I like to think that the brave steps we each take toward accepting our body and loving it will make the path a lot easier for the young women that come after us."

"You're so right, Samantha. I'll remember that. Every time I get scared, I'll think of how brave you are and remember to be brave too."

"That's wonderful." I smiled. My heart pounded. After this conversation I knew that there was only one thing I could do. If I asked the women who read my books to be brave, I had to be brave too.

CHAPTER 19

After the woman walked away, Cateline walked up to me. "I see you're tenderhearted." She grinned.

"It's hard not to be. I'm really surprised by the turnout and the reaction, to be honest."

"You shouldn't be, Samantha. I have to admit your book is one of my favorites on the tour. It's just so honest, that's what I think I like most about it. And you did a great job. When you're ready we'll sit down for autographs, but remember, we want these women to come back for the question and answer session, so do your best to keep the conversations short, okay?"

"I will." I nodded.

As I signed books for each of the women in the audience, I caught sight of Max across the room from me. He was surrounded by a few women and chatted easily with them. It occurred to me that Max had a lot of impact on my life. That he had given me the room to blossom when I needed it—first as my friend, and then as my lover. He caught me looking in his direction and smiled. Then he turned back to the women. I wondered about the idea of including Max in my next book as a way to offer a male's perspective.

I signed the last book and Cateline walked over to me. "I'm sorry we went almost an hour late. Your hand must be sore!"

"A little." I grinned.

"I have a surprise for both of you, but you'll have to rush now, and I'm sorry for that."

"What is it?" I glanced at Max and then back at Cateline.

"I wanted you both to have a chance to experience the Riviera. I have a small cottage there. It's nothing like the huge fancy homes of the wealthy people that live there, but it is a two-minute walk from the water. I took the liberty of buying you two tickets and your flight leaves in just about two hours." She held out a key to me. "I want you to have fun."

"Wow! Cateline, that's too much." I shook my head.

"Please, I wanted to do it. It's the beginning of the tour, and you should get to celebrate." She pressed the key into my hand. "Get some rest and enjoy your days off, alright?"

"Thanks Cateline—for everything."

Max and I headed home from the bookstore to pack for our flight to St. Tropez.

"You must be tired." He reached over and rubbed my wrist.

"No, actually, I'm excited. I just had my first reading and it wasn't a disaster! Now we're going to jet off to a cottage on the beach."

"And you learned that you could do the splits." Max grinned.

The car dropped us off at the bed and breakfast.

"I'll wait for you." The driver nodded to us.

Once we were in our room, I changed out of my air-conditioned pants. I hung up Agnes' blazer in a special spot in the closet. It had become like a talisman for me—a culmination of all of the support and love I had from my fans.

I threw a few things into a smaller suitcase. Max added some of his own too.

"Ready?" He grinned.

"I think so."

"Well, you'd better be, because we can't miss our flight. The car is waiting."

We rushed back out to the car and made the drive to the airport. The plane we took was much smaller than the first, and the flight was short—just enough time for me to catch a quick nap.

When we landed, we made our way to the train station and our final destination of St. Tropez.

The cottage was not hard to find despite the fact that it was dark by this time. My heart raced as I wondered if the key would work. What if she gave me the wrong one? But it turned easily in the lock.

We explored the quaint cottage, then I flopped down on the small couch. "I think it's important for me to start learning some Italian."

"But I thought you were working on French?" Max settled beside me on the couch.

"I was. I still am, but if we're going to Italy next, I think I should know at least some simple phrases."

"I guess you're right." Max grinned. "Just be careful what you're repeating."

"Good point—wouldn't want to run into that man from the plane again."

I searched on my phone for an app to learn Italian. This time I read the description word for word along with the reviews. Once I was satisfied that I knew what the app was all about, I downloaded it. A few minutes later, Italian flooded my ears. I had to admit that Max was right. Even though French was a lovely language to listen to, Italian had a more passionate sound.

I stood up and paced back and forth in front of Max. I repeated the phrases as I did. Now and then I would slip into French and then correct myself and return to Italian. Out of the corner of my eye, I noticed Max's eyes as they followed me back and forth across the room.

I imagined myself speaking to an Italian woman who needed some assistance from my style of inspiration. As I envisioned our conversation, I closed my eyes and suddenly felt Max's hands on my hips.

"Max!" I jumped and turned to face him as I pulled

my headphones off.

"I'm sorry." He bit my neck with playful firmness. "How can you expect me to resist you when you're prancing around speaking French and Italian? I am only a man, Sammy." He offered me a look of hunger.

I resisted laughing at the heat in his eyes. He was serious, and I didn't want to ruin the mood.

"Well, they are they the languages of love, right?"

"I think we should invent our own." He kissed me. "Care to practice it with me?"

"Always." I returned his kiss and dropped my phone.

As we made our way to the bed, Italian phrases surrounded us.

CHAPTER 20

I woke to a light tickle along my naked shoulders. I'd fallen asleep without a stitch of clothing on. When I opened my eyes I saw Max. He stared at me with a subtle smile on his lips.

"Morning." I smiled. "You look like you're thinking about something."

"I am."

"What is it?"

"How I can't wait to see you on the beach like this. It's going to be so much fun to be able to hug you and feel your skin in the water."

The thought of the topless beach made my heart lurch. I still wasn't sure if it was something that I could handle.

"It will have to wait until tomorrow. I really need to get some work done today, and so do you, right?"

"Yes." He sighed. "But tomorrow, promise?"

"I promise."

"Why don't we go out to dinner tonight? Remember, we promised that we'd try something new and strange in every country."

"Alright, that sounds good."

Max crawled out of bed.

I lingered a bit and tried not to think about my bee stings. They didn't hurt as much, but they were still there.

The reading the night before had opened my eyes to the importance of my words. Before, I saw my writing as just something I did and some people enjoyed. Now I understood that it was more than that. I almost had a responsibility to my readers to make sure that the next book was ready to go as soon as possible.

I took a moment to clear my mind and focus on the moment. Then I climbed out of bed.

Max was already showered and dressed so I took a long shower and practiced the technique that Zara used in the book. I soaped my body not just to clean it, but to value it. The more I took care of my body, whether through diet, exercise, or hygiene, the more I showed it gratitude for being my vessel in life.

I took the time to whisper my affection to my skin, to my hips, to the slope of my calves. I spent extra time expressing gratitude for my cheeks and forehead, which were still dotted with bee stings. Then I let the water rinse away and visualized being cleansed from the inside out.

The last thing I did was to turn my face under the spray of the shower. It washed over me and I ignored the sting of it. Instead, I focused on every tiny drop that struck me. Each one was a tiny portion of the full stream.

Each one existed for the sole purpose of rushing across my skin. It was a surreal moment to bond and express gratitude for the water that poured forth.

When I turned the water off I stepped out of the shower and grabbed a towel. My smile brightened as I was preparing for the day ahead.

I dressed and grabbed my computer.

"Ready to go?" I grabbed Max's hand as he walked up to me.

"Sure. You don't want breakfast?"

"We'll grab something at the cafe. I want to eat light so I can splurge tonight."

"We have to find one first."

"I'm sure if we walk a bit, we'll run into one."

We left the cottage behind and walked in the direction opposite the beach.

When I noticed a bed and breakfast on the corner, I thought about Poppy and her husband. They were strange to me in many ways, but they were a perfect fit for each other. They understood one other, and each other's dreams. I had that with Max too. I gave his hand a squeeze.

"I love you."

"I love you too, Sammy." He touched his forehead to mine and then kissed the tip of my nose.

Just as he pulled away I caught sight of a man walking toward us. On the off chance that he might speak English I held up my hand to get his attention.

"Excuse me, sir, sorry to bother you. We're new to the area. Can you direct us to a cafe where we can use Wi-Fi?"

"Sure, just about all of them have it. I'll give you directions to one I know." He sketched out a quick map and handed it to Max.

We thanked him, then followed the map to the street he'd marked.

There was only one cafe on the street, and it was small, but cute. When we stepped inside it was even smaller. The tables were arranged to provide privacy but not quite big enough to sit two people with two computers.

"Do you want to go to another place?" Max pointed to one of the tables. "It's a tight fit."

"No, it's fine. We can work at separate tables. I'll be able to focus better on my own anyway."

"Okay." He nodded and selected a table.

I chose one a few seats away from him.

There were a few other customers in the cafe, all engrossed in their own computer screens. A grungy teenager leaned against the counter and flipped through his phone. It was clear that most people didn't come here for the coffee. Those that spoke did so in French.

It was the perfect place to work on the next chapter of my new book. I wanted to experience being absorbed into another culture in the hope that it would give me a fresh perspective on my writing.

As I waited for the flow to begin, I glanced over at Max. He was hunched over his computer hard at work. It warmed my heart that all of that dedication was for us. I couldn't think of a better way to earn a living than to do it together.

With his hard work to inspire me, I started to get some ideas for the chapter.

As I began to type away, I overheard snippets of conversations around me, the rhythm of the speech immersing me even more in the new ideas that came to me.

Life wasn't about countries, or states, or cities—it was about being open to explore. Not even language and culture should be barriers.

My fingers flew across the keys.

Not long after my flurry began, I had to come up for air.

CHAPTER 21

I looked over at Max and noticed that he was no longer alone. In fact, a beautiful woman was sitting right beside him. She sat so close that she could have easily crawled into his lap.

Max continued to stare at the screen, but I could hear the woman speaking to him. I understood enough of her words to know that they were flirty.

Max glanced up at her and smiled. Why wouldn't he smile? She was gorgeous. Her lips were painted dark red and lined in a way that made them pop. She leaned those lips close to my husband.

"I just love your accent. Keep talking." She scooted closer to him on her chair.

"Ah, I'm sorry, but I really do have some work to do."

She giggled. "So cute."

Max tapped on the keyboard. I didn't want to play the jealous wife card. He wasn't doing anything wrong. He certainly wasn't encouraging her attention.

Every time she leaned close to him I wanted to leap

off my chair and tackle her.

"What are you working on?" She touched his shoulder and leaned so near his cheek that she might have left a smudge of her lipstick behind.

Max's hand flew across the keyboard as he slid back his chair to create some distance between them.

"I don't mean to be rude, but I'm really trying to focus on work."

"You can take a little break for me." The woman batted her long dark eyelashes.

I swallowed hard and tried to remind myself that Max could take care of himself. I couldn't help but wonder if he was attracted to her. Sure, he was being loyal, but that didn't mean he wanted to be. He knew I was right there, after all; would it have been different if I weren't?

"Oh, you Americans." The woman shook her head and walked off.

Max slid his chair back up to the table and looked over at me. He winked, then looked back at his computer.

I was still feeling unsettled.

I had good reason to be, because a moment later, the woman returned with a frothy drink for Max and sat back down beside him. I was floored, not only by her persistence when Max clearly showed no interest, but also by her blatant blindness to the wedding ring he wore. If she knew he was married, why was she going after him?

I watched a moment longer as Max did his best to politely decline the drink. When she tried to insist, I'd had enough. I stood up and walked over to the table. I set my hand down on the table with my wedding band in full view. Then with my best attempt at speaking French, I told her to scram.

She tilted her head to the side with a confused pout and then shrugged.

As she walked away Max looked up at me and tried to hide a smile.

"What?"

"You're so cute when you're jealous."

"I wasn't jealous."

"Oh, no?"

"Not at all. It's about respect, Max. What if some guy hassled me like that? Would you really sit there and watch?"

"No, definitely not. But I also wouldn't ask him if he wanted me to take his dog for a walk."

"What?"

"That's what you asked."

"Was it really?" I groaned. "Oh, I just can't get the hang of these languages."

"It's fine, Sammy, it takes most people years to learn a new language."

"I guess you're right. Are you ready to grab some lunch?"

"Sure."

We found a small cafe where we could get some

sandwiches. "I still want to eat light. What do you think we should try tonight?"

"I have an idea in mind."

"What is it?" I grinned.

"I want it to be a surprise."

"Oh, that's not fair."

"Sure it is, you can pick what we try in Italy. Here, I get to pick. How does that sound? That way we really have to be daring."

"Oh boy, I'm not sure if I can trust you." I laughed.

He set his sandwich down and met my eyes. "You don't mean that, do you?"

"Max, don't be silly."

"I'm sorry, I just want to make sure that you know you can trust me. It's nice to check in once in a while."

"Well, there's no need. I love you and I trust you."

He smiled and took a bite of his sandwich. I took another bite of mine just before my phone started beeping with text messages.

"Are you going to check?" Max tilted his head toward my phone.

"No way, we're eating." I took another bite of my sandwich. Then my phone rang.

"Someone's trying to reach you."

"I better see who it is." I pulled out my phone and saw that it was Cateline. I picked it up quickly. "Hello?"

"Samantha, I've been trying to reach you."

"I'm sorry. Max and I were eating lunch. Is everything

okay?"

"It's really not, Samantha. I'm sorry to say this but I'm disappointed that you released that portion of the book without telling me first. I really don't see how it's going to help the book tour, and, in fact, I'm worried that it may drive some fans away. I'm all for honesty, but this takes it a little too far, I think."

"I'm sorry, Cateline, I don't understand. What are you talking about?"

"On your website—where you released that portion of your new book."

"But that's impossible. The book isn't even complete and hasn't been edited. I didn't release anything."

"I think you'd better take a look at your website, Samantha. I'm afraid there might have been a mix-up."

"I'll take a look and call you back."

CHAPTER 22

I hung up the phone and looked across the table at Max.

"Is something wrong?" Max frowned.

"Cateline said there's a portion of my new book on the website."

"That's impossible. I just updated it this morning." Max shook his head. "I didn't put anything new up."

"Max, we have to take a look at it. She insists it's up there."

Max slid his food out of the way and put his computer on the table in front of him. He popped it open and went through the process of logging in.

My heart pounded as I waited for the verdict. It couldn't be true; it had to be some kind of mistake.

"How did this happen?" Max stared at his computer.

I stood up and walked around the table to look at the screen. As Cateline said, there was an incomplete unedited portion of the new book up on the website.

Even worse, there were notes in between the passages that were never meant to be seen by my readers. They were little notes I made about whether to change the section, expand it, or even delete it. Many included personal thoughts about the passages, or even the experiences in my own life that led me to write them.

None of it was meant to be seen by my readers.

"Max, how did this happen?" I blinked back tears. "Get it off, please!"

Max's fingers flew across the keys. He winced. "I can't."

"What do you mean you can't?"

"There's no Wi-Fi here now. I can't get into the website again. We have to get somewhere with a signal."

My phone started to ring. I knew it was Cateline. I glared at the screen, then answered the phone. "Hello?"

"Did you see it?"

"Yes, Cateline. We're working on fixing it right now. I'm so sorry. It was not intentional."

"Well, it's not a mishap we can let go. You have to get it cleaned up and fast."

"We're trying, I promise. I'll update you when it's fixed." I hung up the phone and looked at Max. "What are we going to do?"

"We have to get back to the cottage. I can fix it there."

"Let's go. Right now, Max!" I knew my tone was harsh, but I was embarrassed. I grabbed my things and we hurried out of the cafe. I tried to hail a cab but none slowed down.

"Now what?" I resisted throwing my phone at a passing cab.

"We'll have to walk. It's not that far."

"Are you sure you know the way?"

"I'm pretty sure. Sammy, I promise I'll fix this."

"But there's no way to fix it, is there?" I started to walk down the sidewalk.

Max caught up with me. "What do you mean?"

"I mean that people have seen it, have read it, maybe even reposted it. There's no way to stop that. I just don't understand how this happened."

"I don't either." Max shook his head. "I didn't do it on purpose. I didn't even open that file."

Suddenly I stopped in the middle of the sidewalk. "But you were distracted, weren't you?" I turned to look at him. I could feel the heat in my own eyes as I stared at him. "If you hadn't been so busy with that hot little latte, you wouldn't have made the mistake."

"Sammy, I know you're upset, but that's uncalled for." Max stopped and turned back to look at me.

"Is it really? Because you were the one who couldn't be bothered to just tell her you were married and shoo her away. I guess you were enjoying her attention a little too much."

"Sammy." Max snaked his hand back through his hair and shook his head. "This is ridiculous. I made a mistake. I'm sorry. I don't know how it happened."

"Well, I do. It happened because you couldn't take

your eyes off of her long enough to pay attention to what you were posting. Maybe if you did, you would have seen the mistake that you were making."

"Sammy, arguing about it isn't going to fix it. Let's just get back to the bed and breakfast."

CHAPTER 23

I sulked along behind Max. I tried to get control of my emotions, but I couldn't. If Max had simply made a mistake it would be one thing, but he made the mistake because he was distracted by a beautiful woman.

And I certainly wasn't feeling very beautiful myself lately. My insecurity was rearing its ugly head. What kind of impression had this made with Cateline? And what about my Italy contact, Isabella? I hadn't even met her and already I would have to explain myself.

Max stayed a few steps in front of me to give me some space. As I stared at his slumped shoulders my chest ached. It hurt him to let me down and I wasn't making it any easier by being so angry.

"Max, let's just stop to get directions. I don't want to get lost."

Max spun around and frowned. "That's just it, isn't it? You don't trust me. You didn't trust me when that woman was flirting with me, you don't trust me when I tell you it was an honest mistake, and now you don't trust me to get us back to the cottage."

"That's not true, Max. I do trust you." I sighed. "There's no time to talk about this now. We have to get back and fix this."

We made our way back to the cottage without getting lost—and without speaking.

Max set up his computer as soon as he was inside the room.

I paced back and forth behind him while his fingers flew across the keyboard.

"There. Okay. It's gone." He pushed the computer back away from him and stood up. "You can take a look."

I sat down in his chair and looked over the website. It was back to normal. I sent Cateline a text to confirm it. When I turned around to face Max he was staring out the window.

"Thank you."

"I'm sorry for making a mistake. I'll be more careful. If you want to hire someone else to do the job, I'll understand."

"Max, I don't want to hire anyone else." I walked up to him and ran my hands along his shoulders. "I'm sorry. I got upset."

"You had a right to be. I'm upset too." He turned around to face me. "Sammy, I would be fine with you being angry at me about the mistake—it was a huge mistake. But the idea that I made it because I was interested in that woman is—"

"Wrong." I met his eyes. "I would have been distracted by her too. She was persistent and disruptive. If you made the mistake, it had nothing to do with you being attracted to her, and it was wrong of me to accuse you of that."

"I'm sorry. I let you down." He shook his head.

"Hey, we're going to be working together for a long time. Mistakes are going to happen on my part and your part. I should have handled this better, and I'm sorry that I didn't. You're right, I'm feeling insecure, and it's making me a little paranoid."

"That's why I want to take you out to the beach, Sammy. I want you to remember to be proud of yourself."

"It's hard here." I bit into my bottom lip.

"Why?" He brushed my hair back from my face and looked into my eyes. "Why would it be hard here?"

"You saw that woman today, Max. That's how most of the women in France look. Sure, I've lost some weight, but I don't look like that."

"Sammy, you were more beautiful than that woman the day I met you, and three years after I met you, and today, as I stand in front of you. Comparing yourself is something you worked hard to leave behind. Don't let it steal your pride or confidence."

I sighed and rested my head against his chest. "If only I could transplant your brain into mine."

"I don't know if I'm ready for that deep a

commitment." Max laughed. He wrapped his arms around me and held me so tight that I could feel the ripple of his muscles. "I love you so much. I don't want to fight. I made a mistake and I'm sorry. But I promise you, it won't happen again."

"I know it won't. It's not a big deal."

"So, we can still go out for my surprise dinner selection?"

"Oh yes, I wouldn't want to miss that."

"Do you want me to call Cateline and apologize?"

"I don't think that's necessary. Let's just let it go. She'll be happy that it's done. The truth is, if we're going to do this, we're going to have to make sure we have our workspace and our time to work ironed out. It's great to experience what the places we visit have to offer, but I don't want to lose ground on getting my next book out. I want to make sure that our focus stays sharp."

"I agree. We can have work days and play days. But tomorrow is definitely a play day."

"I know, I know. The beach." I managed a smile.

Max leaned in close and kissed me.

I pulled away with a sigh. "I should try to get a little work done before dinner."

"Alright, I'll make myself scarce so that I don't distract you." He slipped out of the cottage.

That afternoon I got quite a bit of work done. It wasn't too hard to get swept up with Zara and the other characters of my book when I was already feeling adventurous. By the time Max returned, it was late enough to head out for dinner.

"What did you do while you were out for so long?" I grinned as I grabbed my purse.

"I scoped out the beach and wandered a little."

"Did you see any topless ladies?"

"Actually no, but I did see a perfect place to enjoy the sun."

"I'm glad that you had fun. So what are you planning for tonight?"

"It's a surprise, remember?" His eyes gleamed.

I gritted my teeth and smiled.

CHAPTER 24

The restaurant that Max chose was small, but fancy. There were many paintings hung on the wall of different landscapes around France. While Max ordered, I studied them. It wasn't until I heard what he'd ordered that I turned to look at him.

"We'll both have the escargot, please." He handed the waiter the menus.

"Max." I stared across the table at him. "You can't be serious."

"What do you mean?" Max frowned. "You said you were up for trying something new."

"New, yes, but Max, escargot?" I shook my head. "Isn't that snails?"

"Just don't think about it." He smiled. "Millions of people consider it a delicacy. It can't be that bad."

I opened my mouth to argue, but I knew there was no point. Max had his mind made up and I wasn't going to get out of it.

When they brought out the dish, even the smell of it made my stomach churn—actually, I'm not sure if that was in actuality or in my imagination, but I know my stomach was in knots. I tried to remind myself that sophisticated well-traveled people adored escargot. I needed to try something new. I needed to step out of my comfort zone.

I poked it with my fork and shuddered.

"Oh, this looks delicious. I can't believe we've never tried this before." Max gushed over the presentation of the meal.

I narrowed my eyes as I looked across the table at him. "It's snails."

"Open your mind, Sammy. It may be delicious. You don't know until you try."

"Alright, alright." I poked my fork at the food. I didn't want to try it. I didn't even want to smell it. What I wanted was to find a way to get a different meal without Max finding out.

Max dug his fork in and held up a portion of the food.

"Your turn." He smiled. "We're going to do this together."

"Seriously?" I frowned. "Fine." I jabbed my fork into one of the snails on my plate. I might have stabbed it a little too hard, because a fountain of butter and garlic sauce sprayed across the table and right unto Max's cheek.

"Sammy." He grinned and grabbed a napkin. "Starting food fights, I see."

"Sorry." I glanced around at the other diners, who

didn't seem to notice what had happened.

"That doesn't mean that you're getting out of it. Ready?" He raised his fork in the air.

"How about a toast?" I raised my fork in the air as well.

"Stalling, hm? Okay. To trying new things and experiencing new places."

We clinked forks and then I tucked the food into my mouth.

The butter and garlic sauce awakened my taste buds just enough that they could be tortured by the foreign taste of the escargot. I tightened my mouth to keep from spitting it out.

I was at a fancy restaurant in France. I could not spit my food onto my plate. At least that's what I told myself.

I looked across the table at Max, who looked rather green himself. He didn't chew or swallow. Our eyes met and we both picked up our napkins at the same time. I don't think we fooled anyone when we dug the food out of our mouths and politely tossed the napkins down on our plates.

"Burgers?' Max raised an eyebrow.

"Yes, please." I gulped down my glass of water to get the taste out of my mouth. I drank the water so fast that it hit the back of my throat hard. I started to cough. There was nothing to choke on but water. I still couldn't catch my breath.

I stood up from my chair to try to clear my airway.

Max stood up as well but not before a waiter got hold of me. He must have assumed that I was choking because his arms went around my waist and he began pumping his fists into my stomach. I couldn't even speak to tell him to stop because his very passionate thrusts forced all of the air out of me.

"She's okay, I think she's okay." Max tried to pry me out of the waiter's arms.

The waiter only responded to him in French and continued to thrust into my stomach.

I realized that he wasn't going to stop until he thought he had dislodged something. I made a retching sound and gulped. The man finally released me.

Everyone in the restaurant applauded. The waiter took a bow. I offered him a smile of gratitude.

Max tossed some money down on the table to cover the meal and we rushed out of the restaurant.

"Are you okay?" Max turned to look at me once we were outside.

"I think so." I laughed. "I might have a few broken ribs."

"That's not funny."

"It's a little funny."

"Okay, it is." He laughed. "Let's go find some food we can actually eat."

We spent the rest of the night eating our burgers and laughing about our attempt at enjoying escargot.

CHAPTER 25

Early the next morning Max woke me.

"Beach time. No excuses." He tugged me up out of bed.

I trudged into the bathroom. I pulled on my bathing suit.

During the short walk down the path to the beach, I tried to have a good attitude.

Once my toes were in the sand, I perked up a little. The sun and water were quite inviting.

"Let's go." Max smiled. His smile stretched at the edges. He reminded me of a kid about to open a present.

My heart raced. Was I really going to do this?

The sand was hot against the bare soles of my feet. I started to hop from one foot to the other.

"It's hotter than I expected." Max frowned. "Here, let's stop here." He spread out the blanket so I could cool my feet off.

I hopped right on to it and sighed with relief.

"It's too hot, maybe we should go."

"No way." Max folded his arms across his toned chest and eyed me up and down. "We're not going anywhere. You promised."

"I promised that I would go to the beach." I smiled. "I'm here."

"Sammy, what are you so afraid of?" He caught my hips with the palms of his hands and gazed at me. "I'm shirtless too, you know."

"That's not the same, and you know it." I took a moment to admire him.

"Shouldn't it be? I mean, think about it. Why is it okay for men to parade around in nothing but shorts, but women are expected to cover up? I'm very proud of your breasts, Sammy. I do, however, think they could use a little sun."

"Max, you're not making this any easier." I blushed.

"Alright, alright. Why don't we play in the water a bit?" He grabbed my hand before I could answer and pulled me toward the edge of the water.

I followed after him. "But what about sunscreen? What about my hair?"

"Sh." Max tugged me into the waves that crashed against the shore. "This is supposed to be fun, remember?"

"Okay, I remember." I splashed at him by sloshing my foot through the water.

He laughed and jumped back from the splash. I lunged toward him, but he was too quick. He grabbed me around the waist and lifted me up out of the water.

"Max, no! Put me down! What are you doing?" I gasped.

"Three, two, one, launch!" Max tossed me through the air and into the water.

I was shocked that he was able to hurl me so easily. But when I re-entered the water the impact of the waves was enough to cause my bikini bottoms to slide down my hips. Lucky for me they caught around my thighs. I tugged them up as fast as I could.

As I swam away from Max, it seemed that the bottoms were not quite on right. I tried to straighten them. They still seemed off.

"Max!"

"What's wrong?" He swam up next to me.

"What's wrong with my swimsuit?" I tugged at the waistband. "Something doesn't feel right."

Max looked down into the water. "Did you put something in there?"

"What?" I glared at him. "Of course not."

"Hm." Max grabbed the waistband and tugged it away from my skin. "Are you sure? It looks like something is stuck inside."

"Max, this isn't funny." I splashed him. "Are you trying to get me to freak out and rip off my bottoms?"

"Sammy, it's moving!"

"It is not!" Then I gulped. There was an unmistakable flutter against my cheeks. I didn't care who saw me, I jerked down my bottoms. "Get it out! Get it out! Max, get it out!" I jumped up and down in the water, which provided anyone on the beach with a clear view of my rear end peeking up out of the water with each leap.

If anyone hadn't noticed, my squeals drew their attention. Max scooped his hand between my legs and a tiny fish swam free of my swimsuit and off into the water.

"There aren't any more, are there?"

"No, you're fish-free." Max laughed.

I was not amused. I was mortified. I ran for the beach. I didn't want to be in the water with bikini-invading fish any more. I climbed the sand to our blanket and then sat down on it. Then I draped the sides of it over me.

I wanted to hide. I wanted to disappear. All I knew for sure was that I was not about to remove any other part of my bathing suit.

Most of the people on the beach returned to their relaxation. I wasn't more than a memory to them—one that they'd probably share amidst laughter and wine with friends one day.

Max stared at me from the water. I expected him to come up and join me on the beach. Instead he swam away. I wondered if I'd upset him. It honestly bothered me that he was so determined to get me to do something I was obviously uncomfortable with.

After about a half hour Max sloshed out of the water and crossed the sand toward me.

"Ready to go?" His voice was tight.

"Yes, please."

"Okay." He held out his hand to help me up.

I managed to get to my feet with the blanket still wrapped around me.

He shook his head but didn't say a word.

When we got back to the cottage he made an excuse to leave. I was left alone to think about what happened.

I decided to write a little to try to get to the bottom of why my beach excursion had ended up with me wrapped up in a blanket. What would I say to a fan of my book that had the same experience?

I slipped into Zara mode and churned out a few inspirational passages. What it came down to was that I was afraid. I was afraid that if I crossed that line I would never be able to hide myself again.

Being overweight for me had been all about being invisible. I dressed nice, but never to grab attention. I blended well, so that no one would point out how big I was. I didn't think that anyone should have to look at me.

It made my heart ache to think that I treated myself that way. What was even worse was that in many ways, I still did it. Maybe I was more confident, but the truth was, I still had the instinct to hide.

That night when Max returned he brought me a special meal and lit a candle.

"I'm sorry I took off. I just wanted some time to clear my head."

"It's okay, Max. I know you need your space. We're working and living together. We have to be okay with giving one another space when we need it."

"You're right, but I don't want you to think I needed time away from you. I just needed some time in my own head."

"I understand."

We shared our meal and he kissed me as usual. But I noticed some distance. I didn't think I imagined it.

As we prepared for bed I paused beside him.

"Max, are you upset with me?"

"No."

"It's okay if you are."

"I'm not."

"I'd rather talk about it than sweep it under the rug."

"There's nothing to sweep, Sammy, it's fine. I'm sorry I pushed you so hard. It's your body and your choice to do with it what you want. I shouldn't have made such a big deal out of it."

"I'm sorry, Max."

"Sweetheart, don't apologize to me." His lips were warm as he kissed me. When he pulled away he looked into my eyes. "I love you, Sammy—even if you won't go topless for me." He cracked a smile.

I smiled back.

CHAPTER 26

Even though Max claimed he wasn't mad, when he rolled over with his back to me it was the first time that he hadn't held me as we fell asleep since we'd gotten married. I had let him down, not because I broke a promise, and not even because I hadn't taken my bikini top off, but because I didn't trust him enough to confide how uncomfortable I was feeling. I sighed and closed my eyes.

I tried to force myself into sleep. But my mind raced too fast to allow it. So much flickered through my thoughts, from the anticipation of Italy to the disappointment of my beach excursion.

When I finally fell asleep, I slipped right into a dream.

I stood in front of a crowd of women. I blinked a few times. I couldn't remember how I'd gotten there, or what I was supposed to be doing. I looked down at the podium. Instead of a book, I saw a picture of the beach that Max and I had visited.

When I looked out at the audience, I realized that

there was something very odd about the people that I saw. They all had the same face. It took a moment before I recognized the face. Every person in the audience had their hand in the air to ask a question. I had no idea how I would answer all of their questions. Before I could call on any person, they all began to ask the same question.

"How can you be brave? How can you be brave?"

I gulped and stumbled back from the podium. The floor turned into deep sand. The more I tried to run, the deeper I sank into it.

I woke up with a jolt to find that I'd kicked the blanket off the bed and gotten my feet tangled in the sheets. Max must have turned over in his sleep, because he was snuggled up close to me. I gulped down a few breaths of air.

I was glad that it was just a dream, but as I thought about it, I realized that it was a dream that I needed to have. I sat up in bed, fully aware of what had to be done.

I gave Max's shoulder a shake. "Max."

"Mm?"

"Get up, Max."

"Okay, let me wake up." He started to pull me closer.

"No, Max, I want to go back to the beach."

"Huh?" He opened his eyes.

"Please, Max, I need to do this."

"You don't have to do it for me, Sammy."

"No, I need to do it for me. If you don't want to go, I understand."

"I wouldn't miss it." He climbed out of bed.

We hurried, half asleep, to grab the things we needed. We were still groggy when we stepped out the door and followed the short path to the sand.

Max lingered a few steps behind me as I walked out onto the beach. With the way the waves and the sand pulled me, it was more like I was being led. I stepped up onto one of the highest sand dunes.

My heart raced. My mind flooded with all the reasons that I shouldn't do it. But I ignored them all. I drew a deep breath of the salty air and reached behind my back. I tugged the tie of my bikini until it loosened and released.

The cups of the bikini still clung to my breasts. My breasts that had been through so much—being too small, then too big, then way too big. My breasts that sagged a bit when I lost weight and never fit just right into a sundress. My breasts that had faint stretch marks and odd patches of skin.

They'd endured years of abuse from me as I told them that they weren't good enough, that they'd never be good enough, that I'd have to have surgery if I had any hope of ever feeling comfortable with them. Now that I thought back on the amount of time I stared with hatred at my breasts in the mirror, I realized how silly it was.

My breasts were always perfect.

They were me—the result of my life, and my choices.

I peeled back the cups of the bikini top until it hung down across the rounding of my stomach. My breasts were exposed to the sun, as it shone brighter, and the salty air, which seemed to caress them.

As my eyes closed, I experienced the embrace of nature as it worshiped my physical form the same way that I worshiped the sunrise as it spread before me. I was as much a masterpiece of nature as the ripple of the water, or the expanse of the sky. My heart filled with such freedom that it seemed to float in my chest, giving me the illusion that I could fly if I tried hard enough.

I heard footsteps approach me and slowly opened my eyes. To my surprise, the beach was crowded. A few people looked in my direction. A man snapped a photograph. Normally I'd have been horrified, but instead, I was flattered.

Max took my hand in his and drew my attention. "You look like a goddess in the sunlight." He smiled at me.

"I'm not, I'm just me." I tugged his hand. "Let's go for a swim."

We ran down to the water and splashed into it. The sensation of the cool water against my skin was delightful. Max and I swam in the water for a long time. Peace washed over me just as the waves did.

By the time we left the water I was comfortable with walking along the beach with no top on. I noticed that a few other women had taken their tops off. Whether they did that because I'd done it, or it had always been their intention, I didn't know. I liked to think they might have experienced the same inspiration that I'd known.

Max grabbed a towel and wrapped it around me. It seemed more like an excuse to hold me, which he did. He placed a kiss on my forehead and looked into my eyes. "I love you, Sammy. Can you believe that this is our life?"

I smiled in return. "I love this too. I love the adventure, and the travel, and us being together. But I'd feel like the luckiest woman in the world, no matter where we were, as long as I'm with you."

We kissed for some time as the waves crashed in the distance. The intimacy between us warmed my heart and made everything else disappear.

CHAPTER 27

After Max and I took a quick shower in the cottage, we shared a meal. It was a combination of cheeses, fruit, and yogurt. It was delicious, much better than the awful food we'd tried at the restaurant.

"Here, catch." I tossed a piece of cheese at Max. It bounced right off his nose and landed on his plate.

"Are you trying to start a food fight with me, young lady?" Max scooped up a spoonful of yogurt.

"No! No!" I ducked and tried to avoid any flung yogurt.

Max laughed and ate the yogurt instead. "I'll show mercy this time. But you know not who you mess with."

"Hm, a kind loving man who would never fling yogurt at his wife?"

"Alright, fine. Maybe you do know." He picked up a grape and popped it in his mouth. "So are you ready for tonight?"

"I think so. I guess I'm a little nervous about what questions they might ask."

"Why are you nervous?"

"I don't know. At the reading it was easy because I basically just read a passage from my book. But tonight people will be asking me anything that's on their minds. There's no way to prepare answers for that."

"That's the fun part—the unexpected."

"Maybe for you. You don't have a problem expressing yourself eloquently. I stumble over everything I say, and of course, I tend to blurt out the wrong things."

"You're very articulate *and* you're honest. That's all you need to do well tonight, babe. They're not there to see anyone but you, and they want to hear your honest thoughts and feelings."

"I guess. I'll try to relax. I just hope I don't end up freezing or doing the splits."

"I'll make sure the brakes are on the podium." Max laughed.

We finished our brunch and then headed out to the airport.

The flight back to Paris gave me some time to think about the two days we had left in France. There were so many places that we hadn't had a chance to see in Paris, yet. I looked forward to being able to spend the next day seeing some more of the sights.

But first I had to get through the question and answer session. I just hoped that I wouldn't slip up and say something incriminating.

After we landed, we still had a few hours to kill.

Max glanced at his watch. "Should we call for a car?"

I looked up and down the sidewalk. It was a beautiful day and the streets were packed. "No, let's just roam. I don't want to miss out on the little things that get overlooked by tourists."

"Great. We'll get a little exercise in too."

"Good point."

We held hands as we walked down the sidewalk toward the more populated area. In the middle of all of the congestion I noticed that there were some people riding bicycles. Others were jogging. Even in Paris people were focused on being healthy. When we passed a towering building I looked up at the architecture of it.

"Oh, Max. It's so interesting. I need a picture of this."

I pulled out my phone and let go of his hand. I held up my phone to take a picture. No matter how I angled the phone I couldn't get the entire building in the frame. I took a few steps back and tried again. Still I couldn't get the entire building. I was determined to get the picture.

I moved back farther and farther until I had the entire building in the frame, then I snapped the picture. The moment I took it, I heard horns all around me. They blared so loud that I jumped.

Max, whose attention had been focused on the building, looked toward me. His eyes widened in the same moment that the horns blared. "Sammy, get out of the street!"

I looked around me to see that I'd backed up into the very busy street. Cars swerved and dodged around me. I was in the middle, too far to get back to Max. I turned toward the other side but cars whipped past in that direction as well. I looked for a break in traffic to get across, but no one would stop. They just drove around me with angry glares and sharp gestures. There I was stuck in the middle of the street in the middle of Paris, all because I wanted to take a picture.

Through all of the commotion I heard the high-pitched sound of a bicycle bell.

"Hey, you! Yes, you!"

A woman, who had to be in her seventies, waved to me from the sidewalk. "Listen to my bell. When you hear it, go! Okay?"

I stared at her. Should I risk my life and trust a complete stranger? The woman nodded to me. I decided I wouldn't be any safer by staying in the street. I nodded back to her.

She watched the traffic and after a few minutes rang the bell. I didn't take the time to check for cars, I just ran for her side of the road.

Max tried to dodge the cars to get into the street but none would stop for him. I made it to the edge of the street and scraped my ankle on the curb as I jumped onto it. My heart raced. I looked back at the traffic that sped by and had no idea how I'd survived.

"Thank you!" I turned to the woman who'd helped me. "Thank you so much."

"No need to thank me. Just be more careful."

"I will." I shook my head. "I was just so caught up in the beauty. I don't know how I managed to do something so stupid."

"We all do stupid things now and then. Don't let it trouble you." She leaned close to me. "But if you think that building is beautiful, you must see Sainte Chapelle. I promise you, you won't regret it." She gave my hand a light pat. "Don't worry about how the world sees you, my dear, worry only about the way you see the world." She waved to me and then rode off on her bicycle. She rang her bell a few times as she disappeared into the crowd.

Max jogged up to me and took my hand.

"Are you okay? I'm so sorry—I couldn't get to you. Please tell me that you're okay."

"I'm fine." I laughed, though I was still in a little shock. "I don't know what I was thinking. But I just met the most wonderful woman."

"Really? How can you know she was wonderful if you only talked to her for a moment?"

"I know. She said a beautiful thing to me and told me that we have to see Sainte Chapelle. Can we go? Do you mind?"

"Sure, we can go. But let's call the car service. I think roaming is a bad idea."

"I think you're right about that." I dialed the car service.

CHAPTER 28

When the driver arrived to pick us up, he knew exactly where to go. He dropped us off at the end of a long line.

"Are you sure about this?" Max frowned.

"I have to see it. There's no way that I met that woman by accident."

"Alright." Max took my hand and we waited in line.

It took about half an hour, but when we reached the front of the line I knew that I wouldn't regret it. The majesty of the structure was enough to take my breath away. That, combined with the massive stained glass windows and colorful tiles, gave me the sensation that I'd walked into a dream world.

I heard Max take a sharp breath as we paused in front of the large circular stained-glass window.

"It was worth it, huh?"

"Yes." Max squeezed my hand.

As I stared into the myriad of colors and witnessed the sunlight that streamed through the window, I recognized that whoever had created the masterpiece understood beauty. I knew in that moment that there was such awesome creativity in the minds of mankind, that to limit myself to the idea that there was only one definition of beauty was impossible.

I thought of every person that I'd met as a piece of that large circle, a perfect shimmering flawless section of glass that blended together to create unparalleled beauty.

The impact of the sight stayed with me later that evening, as I dressed for the last of my author events in Paris. I didn't think so much about how I looked in the mirror, but how I looked in my own eyes. Could I see my beauty? Could I see my worth?

I left the bed and breakfast with a different form of confidence growing within me—a certainty that all that I was was exactly what I needed to be.

When we arrived at the question and answer session, many people were already there.

Cateline smiled at me as I stepped inside. "Samantha, you look beautiful."

I understood the compliment. She might have admired my dress, or my hair, but I knew that her compliment was more toward what she saw inside of me. I felt beautiful, not in a shaky forced way, but in a free and accepting way.

"We're just about ready to start if you are. No need to be formal. This is just meant to be a relaxed and comfortable encounter. If anyone makes you uneasy, just nod your head to me and I'll intervene, alright?"

"Okay." I smiled. I remembered the dream I'd had the night before. Now I was prepared to answer anything asked of me, with honesty.

The room was as crowded as it had been at the reading. There were even a few new faces.

I noticed a man in the back of the room with a camera. For a split second I thought it might have been the same man that was on the beach that morning, but I shook the thought away. It couldn't be him. Why would he travel so far?

I turned my attention to the crowd of women who sat before me. "Welcome, everyone. Thank you for being here. I'd just like to say that it means the world to me that you've all enjoyed the book, and I hope you know that it inspires me just to see you here."

There was a small smattering of applause, then women began to raise their hands to ask their questions. A woman stood up near the front of the crowd.

"Samantha, in your book you talk a lot about confidence and loving your body. Do you think that it contradicts these thoughts to be so focused on weight loss?"

I thought about her question for a moment to make sure that I could answer it clearly.

"No, I don't think so. The truth is, we're all beautiful, no matter our size. But I believe our bodies function better at a healthy weight. I believe that if someone is truly confident—that if a woman truly loves her body and moves through whatever issues she may have to deal with at the time—the weight naturally shifts on her body as she works to treat it in loving ways. Now if a woman feels she's healthy and happy with her weight, I think that's wonderful too. My personal goal has always been to be healthy and so that's been my focus."

The woman nodded and sat back down.

I smiled at another woman who waved her hand in the air. "Yes?"

"I recently read the portion of your new book that you released on your website."

"Oh yes, unfortunately that was a mistake. It wasn't meant to be released."

I could see Max grimace in the back of the room.

"I thought it was genius! I loved having a window into your mind. All the books I've read about women and body image—and just life in general—are always so glossy. Everything seems perfect. It was refreshing to see the process that goes into creating those perfectly edited pages. But I did have a question about it."

"What's that?" I smiled.

"When will it be released?"

I laughed. "Well, I have to finish it first, then I'll let you know."

A woman near the back of the room stood up when I nodded to her.

"Samantha, I have a question for you."

"Okay." I smiled.

"Is this you?" She held up a photograph.

CHAPTER 29

My heart jumped as I realized that it was a photograph from that very morning when I stood on the beach topless. The audience fell silent as the woman continued to hold up the photograph. "Is it?"

I looked past the sea of faces to Max, who stood up from the wall and moved toward me.

The other man in the room, the one I recognized from the beach that morning, stepped forward as well.

I took a deep breath and knew there was no way to avoid the truth. "Yes, it is me."

A ripple of whispers carried through the audience.

The woman who held the picture lowered it. "I think it should be your next book cover."

"Oh?" I breathed a sigh of relief. I expected to be raked over the coals for being indecent. "I'm not so sure I could get away with that." I laughed.

"It is a work of art." The man who snapped the picture paused beside the woman. He continued, "Do you mind if I share something with you?"

"Go right ahead." I nodded.

"I was surprised this morning when you did not yell at me for taking your picture. I was prepared to be chased." He pointed to the sneakers on his feet.

Max paused beside him and gave him a look of warning.

"I'm a professional photographer and I just couldn't resist snapping a picture of that moment. Your expression was just—wow!" He shook his head. "I had no idea who you were when I took the picture, but when I showed my wife, she knew who you were." He smiled at the woman who held up the picture. "She insisted we bring it to you—as a gift. After she told me what an impact your book has had on her view of her own beauty, I agreed. In fact, I've started to read your book, and though I know it is targeted toward women, I'm getting a lot from it myself. You're very talented and quite beautiful—and my wife and I would like you to have this portrait."

I stepped down from the podium and walked toward them. As I took the picture that was handed to me, all of the familiar qualms about looking at myself in a photograph rose to the surface.

"How often do we avoid looking at pictures of ourselves when we don't feel that we're perfect?" I looked around at the women in the audience. "This man captured a moment that was life-changing for me, and when I look at this picture, I don't want to tear it down, I want to appreciate it. This is the place we need to get to as women—or men." I smiled at the photographer. "A place where we accept our bodies for the natural beauty that they are. Thank you for this gift."

With a tremble in my hands I lifted the photograph so that everyone in the room could see. I ignored the sweat along my forehead and the way my heart pounded against my chest. "This is me, this is who I am, relaxed and embracing the world around me, without fear of others judging me. This moment will always be precious to me, but it would never have happened if it weren't for the support of all of you—and my husband Max, who always reminds me to be proud of myself. So my challenge to all of you is to go out and experience this. You can have someone photograph it, or not. You can wear a top, or nothing at all, but be brave enough to embrace and display your body for the beauty that it is."

Applause surrounded me as I lowered the photograph. Off to the side of the room I noticed Cateline speaking to another woman. A jolt of apprehension rushed through me as I remembered that Isabella was at the session. I didn't know if the other woman was her, but if it was, had she been offended by my picture?

I handed the photograph to Max and returned to the podium to complete the session. After I answered what felt like hundreds of questions, Cateline took over the podium to close out the evening.

I was a little winded from the event. I didn't realize how much effort it took to speak for a long period of time.

I signed a few autographs for people who hadn't been at the earlier reading. When another book was held out to me to sign, I looked up at the woman holding it. It was the same woman I'd noticed Cateline speaking to earlier.

Cateline came from behind to stand beside me. "Samantha, this is Isabella, the owner of the bookstore in Italy which will be the next stop on the tour."

CHAPTER 30

Isabella had the type of body that made me think of a statue in a museum. It was strong, regal, and rather intimidating. Her features were just as strong, with high cheekbones, wide dark eyes, and flowing thick brown hair. When she looked at me there was a hint of displeasure in her expression as if she needed to be convinced that I deserved to exist.

"Isabella, it's nice to meet you."

"Thank you." She swept her eyes up and down my body and then nodded. "You look well."

"Thank you." I cleared my throat and tried not to show my discomfort with being scrutinized.

"You do know that in Italy we can't have you strutting around without your clothes on, hm?" She arched an eyebrow. "It isn't France, after all."

"Oh sure, of course. No, I'll be sure not to be naked ever. I mean, in public. Not that I was naked here, I was just topless. But I won't be topless in Italy at all. Anywhere."

She stared hard at me. Then her entire body began to shake. I thought I must have said something to upset her and braced myself for the consequences. Instead, she burst out laughing.

"I'm so sorry, I was just teasing you. I think the portrait is beautiful. I just know that you'll have a wonderful time in Italy. I'm looking forward to showing you a few of my favorite places—you and your charming husband." She looked past me and winked at Max.

I glanced over my shoulder at Max, who stood like a deer in headlights. I tried not to grin at his flustered expression. Yes, Isabella was one powerful force, and I was quite curious about what would happen in Italy.

"We would enjoy that, Isabella, thank you for the offer."

"Shall we have a coffee and chat? It's about time to close up," said Cateline.

"That sounds great." I handed the book back to Isabella.

"There's a cafe around the corner. You three go ahead and I'll meet you there once everything is locked up."

"Alright." I nodded.

Isabella smiled. Something about the way she looked at me still left me unsettled. I wasn't sure if it was because her gaze was so intense, or because she saw something she didn't like.

We walked around the corner to the cafe. Once we

were settled at a table we placed our orders. Isabella focused right on me.

"You did a fine job with the question and answer session. You may find that we do things a little differently in Italy. But I think you're going to enjoy it."

"Differently how?"

"I'll tell you when you arrive." She smiled.

Cateline arrived before I could question Isabella further.

"I'll have a coffee, black, two sugars." She sat down between Isabella and me.

"I hate to see you go, Samantha, but I know that Isabella will show you a great time."

I smiled. I was a little concerned about what that might mean.

"I have to say, Samantha, that as I read your book I felt it was a reflection of my own experiences. It was rather surprising. I kind of expected you to look just like me," said Isabella.

I raised an eyebrow. I couldn't quite understand how such a flawless woman expected me to look like her. Without knowing what to say, I only nodded.

"I've been so tall and so much broader than other women all of my life that I find it hard to be confident. But you, you're delicate and beautiful. I don't see how you had such a difficult time. Things must be very different in America."

Delicate? Beautiful? My eyes widened. Could she

really be talking about me? "Isabella, you are gorgeous—I don't see how you could find any imperfection in the way you look."

"Oh, thank you. You're very kind." She waved her hand dismissively.

"No, I mean it."

"Isn't that funny?" Isabella sipped her coffee. "We see each other so differently than we see ourselves."

"It is."

"I find that I spend more time avoiding my reflection than actually looking at it." Cateline shook her head. "I can't remember the last time I was satisfied looking in the mirror. That's why your book is so powerful, Samantha. You make it clear that no matter what a woman's personal health goal is, they're beautiful from start to finish. If only I could find a way to get that to stick in my brain."

"It's not an easy journey."

All three of us looked over at Max, his statement surprising even me a bit.

Max seemed to shift in his chair at the scrutiny. "I mean, I've seen what Sammy has gone through. I think the strangest thing is that no matter how much I tell her how beautiful she is, no matter how much I try to get her to see it, she doesn't always believe me. She's had to work hard to build her confidence and every step has been a struggle. I'm just glad that she's been brave enough to get closer to that knowledge."

"And that she's helping other women to do the same." Isabella smiled. "Maybe one day we'll all be able to believe our lovers when they rave about our beauty."

"I hope so." I took Max's hand under the table.

Isabella glanced at her watch.

"I must be going. I've enjoyed meeting both of you."

"I should get going too." Cateline wiggled her eyebrows. "I have a date."

"I'll let you two enjoy the rest of your time in France. Call me when you arrive in Italy, alright?" Isabella smiled at me.

"Absolutely." I stood up, as did Max, to see them off.

As Isabella and Cateline walked away, I considered myself lucky to have met two amazing women and for all the adventures that awaited us in Italy.

Max wrapped his arm around my waist and pulled me close. "How about a walk in the moonlight?"

I turned to look at him with a wicked smile. "A walk sounds nice—if it's followed by dessert after."

Max grinned and kissed my nose. "Now that sounds like a deal, my love."

A NOTE FROM THE AUTHOR

Fictional character, Samantha Bradford and the Single Wide Female books are written for every woman out there who has struggled with their weight, self-esteem and any number of issues that we all face as we work to become the best versions of ourselves that we can be.

These books are meant to be light-hearted and fun, with the hope that they will also inspire you to make your own "bucket list" of sorts—and to REALLY live your life to the fullest, loving yourself completely as you do so.

Lillianna loves to hear from her readers and can be contacted via her website where you can also download a complimentary book.

LilliannaBlake.com

ALL TITLES BY LILLIANNA BLAKE

Single Wide Female in Love
#1 The Date
#2 The Girlfriend
#3 The Fiancée
#4 The Wife

Single Wide Female Travels
#1 Sammy in France
#2 Sammy in Italy

Other Single Wide Female Titles
My Valentine's Day
St. Paddy's Day Disaster
A Bunny Tale
Sammy's Christmas List

Becoming Zara
*how the B.I.G. Girls Club came to be

B.I.G. Girls Club
The Rockstar's Girlfriend
The Former Model

Visit the author website at LilliannaBlake.com to get on the notification list for new releases and to receive a complimentary book to learn what inspired Sammy to begin her bucket list.